LINE OF FIRE

archer tactical series

A.K. EVANS

ISBN: 978-1-951441-17-3

This is a work of fiction. Names, characters, places, and incidents are the product of the author's imagination or are used fictitiously. Any resemblance to actual events, locales, or persons, living or dead, is coincidental.

Cover Artist
cover artwork © Sarah Hansen, Okay Creations
www.okaycreations.com

Editing & Proofreading
Ellie McLove, My Brother's Editor
www.mybrotherseditor.net

Formatting
Stacey Blake at Champagne Book Design
www.champagnebookdesign.com

DEDICATION

A new series… as always, this goes to my
husband and our two boys.

LINE OF FIRE

archer tactical series

PROLOGUE

Kaia

I TOOK A DEEP BREATH AND PREPARED MYSELF.

Remain calm. Don't let her know.

"Hey, Parker," I greeted my sister as I put the phone to my ear and pushed the blankets back from my body so I could get out of bed. "Does she miss me already?"

My older sister let out a gentle chuckle.

It felt so good to hear that from her. I'd been hearing it more often over the last year any time I spoke to her, and I was convinced there was nothing better.

Well, until a few weeks ago.

"She does," Parker answered. "I don't know how it's possible, but somehow, this little girl knows that her aunt is no longer in the house. There's no question about it. She misses you, Kaia. Then again, she's not the only one."

Warmth spread through me. It had only been three days since I was in Rising Sun, Wyoming, but I missed them so much already. My sister, Parker, had just given birth to my niece, Wren, only three weeks ago. I had planned to be there for the delivery, but Wren decided to arrive a week ahead of schedule.

I'd spent two weeks with Parker, her husband, Nash, and their daughter, Wren. To say I missed them now would have been putting it mildly.

"That's because everyone knows Auntie Kaia is good at handling the night shift," I joked. "I could stay awake all night just watching her sleep."

Parker sighed. "I wish you were still here," she said. "And I'm not just saying that because Nash and I were able to get a couple of hours of uninterrupted sleep."

I couldn't stop myself from smiling. "I know," I replied. "As much as I wish I could have stayed longer, I needed to get back. I still have to work."

"Yeah," Parker murmured. "Well, we're counting down the days until you come to visit again."

I wasn't sure how soon I'd be able to get back out to Rising Sun, but I knew I wouldn't be able to handle long periods away from them.

"I'll figure it out soon and let you know when I can make another trip," I promised.

"We can't wait."

I couldn't either. Though, as much as I wanted to visit with them again, I knew I wouldn't have been ready to go back immediately if yesterday hadn't happened. As quickly as the thought popped into my mind, I pushed it out. I couldn't risk getting myself worked up while I was on the phone with Parker.

"I'm so happy for you, Parker," I declared, attempting to push the conversation back into positive territory. "I know we talked a little bit about it while I was there, but I think it bears repeating just how proud I am of you."

"I know you are," she returned. "Sometimes, I still can't believe this happened, you know?"

"What do you mean? Having Wren?"

There was a moment of silence before she answered, "Not just her—all of it. I mean, I never thought I could have this, Kaia. After everything we've been through, I never imagined life would ever be this good."

There was nothing in this world I wanted more than to know that my sister finally had everything she deserved in her life. She was a successful chiropractor. She was also married to an amazing man who loved her beyond what I ever thought was possible. And now they had their beautiful daughter. Parker was nothing short of an incredible mother, too. I knew she'd give her daughter everything, particularly all the love we never had as kids.

That wasn't entirely true.

Parker and I did have love. We got it from each other. But all we had was one another, and after everything Parker had done for me when we were children, there was nobody on this earth who deserved a happy ending more than my sister did.

"It's long overdue," I noted. "But at least you've got it. I know you'll be forever grateful for it."

"You've got that right," she agreed. "And even though I know you aren't at the same place just yet, I'm certain you're well on your way. It's such a bummer Nolan couldn't come out with you."

I swallowed hard as I sat up in the bed and swung my feet over the side of the bed. Before I stood up, I responded, "Yeah. There was no way he could take off of work for that long. Besides, if he had come out with me, I probably wouldn't have extended my trip for that additional week."

"Well, in that case, I'll just say that I'm glad you made it out and that I hope he gets to come out with you next time," she started. "I'd love for him to meet Wren."

I'll never let that happen, I thought.

When I didn't reply, Parker added, "Maybe once he meets her, it'll make him start thinking about the future with you. I can't wait to be by your side through your engagement, your wedding, and your pregnancy."

Not wanting to alarm her but also not wanting to make it seem like I was even remotely interested in having any of that happen, I tried to lighten my voice before I replied, "I just got this residency at Club Infinity, Parker. I'm not ready for a wedding or a baby yet."

"I know, I know. You've worked so hard to get that residency, too, so I know how important it is to you. And I'm very proud of you. But that doesn't mean I can't hold out just a little bit of hope that you'll be giving me a niece or nephew of my own soon."

I didn't want to dash her hopes, so I stood up from the bed and told her, "I'm sure it'll happen when the time is right."

At least I wasn't lying. Despite everything, I still wholeheartedly believed that.

Just then, I heard Wren in the background. She was getting fussy.

"Oh, no. She's sad," I declared as I started walking toward the bathroom.

"I'm sure she's just ready to eat again," Parker remarked. "I should get going."

"Okay. Give her lots of kisses from me and tell Nash I said hello."

"I will. Love you, Kaia."

"Love you, too."

With that, I stepped into the bathroom and set my phone down on the ledge of the sink. Then, standing in front of the mirror, I allowed my gaze to travel up from my abdomen to my face.

Blood had dried on the bottom corner of my lip, where it had been split open. I might have been able to clean that up and hide it pretty well, but I wasn't sure I'd be as successful with the bruising and swelling on my cheek.

All of it inflicted last night by Nolan.

I wanted nothing more than to call my sister immediately after it happened, but I couldn't. I refused. She had enough to worry about with her three-week-old baby. Not only that, but I knew what would happen if I told her.

Parker had always been the one to jump in to protect me when our father got angry when we were little. She'd saved me enough.

It was my turn to stand on my own and fight for myself.

I just wasn't sure where to start.

But as I stared at myself in the mirror, saw the evidence of my boyfriend's physical abuse, and thought about the precious baby my sister had just brought into the world, I made a promise to myself. I was going to make sure that when my niece grew up, she'd have an aunt who made her proud. She'd have someone she could look up to.

5

And no matter what, she'd know that despite what came her way, she'd always be able to depend on me to be there for her.

Because I'd never, *never* allow myself to be taken away from her.

CHAPTER 1

Kaia

"HEY, KAIA, CAN WE TALK BEFORE YOU HEAD UP?"
I was never more grateful for the fact that I
worked in a dark atmosphere than I was tonight.
And at this very moment, I was even more thankful for it.
Because Mateo wanted to chat.

"Yeah, sure. What's going on?" I responded.

I was secretly praying that all my efforts throughout the
day had paid off. After getting off the phone with my sister
this morning, I spent the remainder of the morning and nearly
all afternoon applying ice to the side of my face. I hoped that
it would help reduce the swelling. I had convinced myself I
was successful and carefully applied some makeup to hide the
evidence of what Nolan did to my face.

Before I left my studio apartment to come into work tonight, which was the first time I'd left since the incident occurred, I checked and double-checked my face. I looked at it
in the lighting of the bathroom, the kitchen, and even near the

windows. When I got to my car, I checked again. I was sure nobody would notice unless they were looking for something.

Luckily, Mateo wasn't looking.

"I know this is last minute, so I'll understand if you can't do it, but I was hoping you'd be able to cover me tomorrow night," he started. "My girlfriend, Aubrey, lives a couple of hours away, but she surprised me last night and showed up at my door."

That was sweet. Mateo was a good dude, and I was glad his girlfriend had done something to make him happy.

Before I could respond to him, Mateo continued, "I completely understand if you can't do it, so please don't feel obligated."

"Not at all," I assured him. Then, and since I didn't have any plans of my own, I confirmed, "I can totally cover you. Is Bianca cool with it?"

Mateo nodded. "Yeah. Then again, I wasn't exactly worried she wouldn't be. I mean, you're Kaia Banks. Everyone loves you."

Not everyone, I thought.

Even still, I smiled at him. "You're too kind, Mateo."

"You're the best, Banks," he replied. "Thank you."

"You're welcome."

"Whenever you need me to cover you, just let me know," he offered.

I wasn't sure I'd be in a position to need him to cover me at any point in the near future, considering this was my life now. Despite that, I said, "I appreciate that."

With that, I excused myself to make my way up to the second floor to meet with Bianca to go over the next month's schedule. Once I made it to her office, I knocked on the door.

"Come in," she called back from behind the door.

I opened the door and walked in.

Bianca grinned at me. "You're back," she declared. "How was the trip?"

Immediately, thoughts of my sister and her family filled my mind. I couldn't stop myself from smiling.

"It was great," I answered. "I had a wonderful time, and Wren is just too precious."

"Oh, I love her name," Bianca marveled. "Do you have any pictures?"

Nodding, I pulled out my phone, navigated to the photos, and held it out to Bianca. She took it from me and swiped through.

"She's so cute. How did you ever leave her?"

I shrugged as I sat down in the chair. "I have no idea," I confessed. "I never knew I could love someone as much as I love my sister, but here I am."

Bianca held my phone out to me and said, "Well, as much as I would have understood your need to stay longer, I'm glad you're back."

"Me too," I told her. "I enjoyed the break and the time off with my sister and her family, but I'm ready to get back to work. How did it go here?"

"It was business as usual," Bianca shared. "Nothing too major to report. As you know, we've got Dawn for Daybreak coming in a couple of weeks, and that's huge for us. A band that big coming to this small town to play for us is a big deal. I've got someone else in the works right now, but there's no guarantee."

"Who?" I wondered.

Bianca's face lit up. She opened her mouth to answer

but stopped herself. "No. No, I'm going to hold on to this for just a little bit longer until it's confirmed. I don't want to jinx anything."

I rolled my eyes. It wasn't like I had anyone I could or would tell the news to anyway. "Oh, whatever," I replied.

"Did you see Mateo?" she asked, quickly changing the subject.

"Yes, he caught me before I came up," I answered. "You're okay with me covering for him, right?"

Bianca gave me a look of indifference. "From a work standpoint, yes," she confirmed. "I'd be stupid not to. But I have to admit I was hoping you'd turn him down for personal reasons."

My brows pulled together. "What does that mean?"

"I thought we'd be able to get together tomorrow outside of work," she started. "In fact, I already talked to Skylar about it, and she said she was up for it, too. We even planned and talked to the husbands, so we were all hoping you and Nolan could join us."

Bianca and Skylar were my closest friends. Admittedly, in my line of work, it hadn't been hard to find people to hang with, but most of the people I'd come into contact with were merely just acquaintances. Bianca and Skylar were more than that. We got together regularly. Or regularly enough that I considered them to be my friends.

While they were both already married, it didn't seem to hinder their need for fun every so often. And for a while, that worked well for me, especially as I found myself needing to acclimate to my new hometown.

I moved from Wyoming to Poppy Valley, California, just over a year ago. It was partly because I wanted a change of scenery but mostly because I knew it would be good for my career. Plus, I needed to know I could do this on my own. Be self-sufficient, take care of myself, and not depend on my sister to always be the one looking out for me.

And I was doing it.

It felt good to know I was capable and strong. None of what I felt had anything to do with me not liking what Parker had done for me over the years. It was more about me feeling the need to be independent while allowing her to live her life and see that she went after what she deserved.

And now that she had it, I knew I'd made the right decision.

Despite where things were for me now, I still didn't regret my choice to come here. Sure, I made one foolish mistake. But I was going to learn from that and move on.

Which is why I needed to share the truth with Bianca. Well, part of it, anyway.

"So, obviously, you know that I'm going to be here working tomorrow night," I began. "But I guess I need to tell you something."

"What's going on?" she asked, tipping her head to the side curiously.

I took in a deep breath before I shared, "I ended things with Nolan."

Bianca's eyes widened. "What? Why? I thought you two were solid," she countered.

Nodding, mostly because I understood her disbelief, I explained, "Yeah, it just… it just isn't going to work out. My trip back to see my sister solidified things."

"Oh, man. I'm so sorry," Bianca lamented.

Shaking my head, I insisted, "Don't be. It's okay. I'm really okay with it. I concluded that it would never really work out for us in the long run. This was truly for the best, and I'm completely at peace with my decision."

"Are you sure?" she pressed.

"Yeah. Definitely."

Bianca's expression turned sad. "I was really rooting for the two of you," she shared. "Who knows? Maybe you'll feel differently after you two have a bit of a break. It was the same for Ken and me in the beginning. We had been dating for three months and decided to take a break. Two weeks later, we realized we were being stupid and hated being without one another."

I wanted to tell her that this wasn't that. Nolan and I had been together for eleven months, and I'd just had a two-week break from him. This wasn't about uncertainty if we were meant to be together. This was all about him proving to me that he was a massive dick by putting his hands on me last night.

Instead of sharing that with her, I said, "I love your hopeful mindset, mostly because I'm the same way about stuff like this. That said, I can promise you that Nolan and I are officially over. There is no chance for a future reconciliation."

Bianca sighed. I wanted to laugh. It was like I'd destroyed all of her hopes and dreams.

"Well, then I'll talk to Skylar, and we'll figure out another time that the three of us can get together without Ken and Cole," she reasoned. "Our sole mission will be to help you get over your heartbreak."

At her statement, I had to fight back the laughter threatening to burst forward. There was no heartbreak here. None.

I wasn't devastated. Nolan was a jerk—an ass—and I had no use for a man like him.

"Keep me posted on what you figure out," I urged her. "As long as I'm not working, I'll be free."

At that, she perked right up. "Perfect. Let's take a look at the schedule for the next month and make sure it's all good for you before you head out there and get the night started for everyone," she suggested.

So, that's what we did.

And ten minutes later, with no changes needing to be made to my schedule, I walked out of Bianca's office and prepared myself for my night ahead.

As I descended the stairs that led down to the main floor, I couldn't help myself from taking in the space. Though I would have had every reason to feel heartbroken, upset, or even angry about what happened last night with Nolan, I didn't.

Because I worked here.

Club Infinity. The premier nightclub in Poppy Valley.

I was living my dream.

DJ Banks. That was me.

Ever since I could remember, music had been an escape for me. When Parker and I were living some of our darkest moments, I turned to music to deal with everything I felt. As time went on, something else sparked inside me. By the time my sister got us out from under our father's abusive thumb, I knew this was what I was meant to do.

And because we'd gone through everything we had, Parker suffering the worst of it, I knew there was nothing else we wouldn't be able to do. If we could survive our childhood, we could do anything.

So, I had been determined.

But the opportunity I had been looking for, the dream I wanted to live, wasn't going to be found in Wyoming. That's why I packed up and left. That's why I was here in Poppy Valley.

It took me some time to get to where I was now, but it was worth it. A couple of weeks after I moved from Rising Sun, I managed to snag a spot opening for another DJ who worked at Club Infinity. It was a small gig, and I only played a few nights a month since the opening acts didn't have contracts. Though I hated not having the consistency I wanted, I knew it would eventually pay off if I stuck with it.

When that DJ took another opportunity in Hollywood two months ago, he left an open residency. I immediately applied for the position. And because I'd pushed so hard and people enjoyed my sets, I got the job.

It was a dream come true.

As an open-format DJ, I could play any genre of music I liked. Of course, coming to work wasn't merely a matter of playing music I liked or felt like listening to at any given moment. It was about so much more.

It was immersing myself in the crowd—in their vibe— and noting what they were doing. I had to read the group, make sure they were enjoying themselves and sticking around until the club closed. Because if I didn't, if I made one wrong move, I could ruin the mood in the air for the rest of the night.

Fortunately, I was good at what I did. I was proud of the job I'd done since taking over the residency, and I was looking forward to seeing what the next several months would bring. It was, by far, the most rewarding job I'd ever had.

Club Infinity had indoor and outdoor space, but I spent

my time indoors unless there was a special event outside. We had VIP lounge seating, state-of-the-art sound and lighting systems, interactive screens, full-service bars, and my home away from home, the DJ booth.

Having made my way across the massive open space, I wasn't surprised to find that it was beginning to fill up with people ready to start winding down from their workweeks. It was a Thursday night, after all. For many people, especially during the summer months in Poppy Valley, the weekend started now.

"There she is."

I looked up and to the left just as I started to climb the five steps that led to my raised DJ booth. Juan was there.

"Here I am," I beamed at one of the club's security members.

"How was the vacation?" he asked.

Nodding, I answered, "It was nice to get away."

"We missed you, Banks," he shared. "It's good to have you back."

"Thanks, Juan. It's good to be back. How have the crowds been?" I asked.

He shrugged. "Not unruly," he replied. "Then again, it's never the same vibe as it is when you're up there." His head jerked toward my booth.

"You know your job is to make sure nobody comes in there and tries to mess with me, right?" I questioned him. "When did they add flattery to your job description?"

Juan chuckled. "You're crazy, Banks. You know you're good."

I liked to think so, but it still felt good to receive the compliment. "Yeah, but it's still nice of you to say so," I told him.

"You know I got your back," he said.

"I do."

And he did.

There had been a total of two instances where Juan had needed to jump into action while I was in the booth, and over-zealous patrons had attempted to climb the stairs and enter it with me. They didn't get very far. Well, other than out the door of Club Infinity, all thanks to Juan's quick reflexes.

I didn't know how he did it, but I'd never seen anyone move the way Juan did on those occasions. Something about how he handled situations where someone needed to be escorted off the property was so different from any of the other bouncers or security I'd seen at other clubs over the years.

Perhaps that was why he was the one in charge of the security team here. They had this uncanny ability to read situations before they got too out of control.

With one last smile and a nod in his direction, I climbed the remaining stairs and entered the booth.

And before I knew it, all that I'd been carrying around with me since last night melted away. Maybe that was strange—I didn't know—but I didn't care. I was in the zone, I was happy, and I was going to enjoy the next few hours for everything they were going to give me.

In fact, I was so into it, I hadn't realized how quickly the hours ticked by. Skylar, who worked as a server, stopped in a couple of times throughout the evening to refill my nonalcoholic beverages. And the next thing I knew, I was packing it in and getting ready to head back home. When I walked out of the booth, I found Juan was still standing in his spot, waiting for me.

"Killer night," he declared.

"Thanks."

"You ready to head out?" he asked.

"Yeah."

Every night I worked, I was escorted out to my car by a security team member. As Juan and I made our way to the exit, I asked, "Are you working tomorrow night?"

"Yep," he replied. "You got plans with your man?"

"Nope. I'm working tomorrow night. Mateo asked if I'd cover for him," I shared. Following a brief pause, I added, "And there's no longer a man."

"No shit?" he asked, stopping in front of the exit that led to the employee parking lot.

"No shit."

"Sorry to hear that, Banks."

"It's all good," I insisted as we stepped out into the well-lit lot.

The owners of Club Infinity took care of their employees, and the safety and security of each member of the staff were of the utmost importance.

A moment later, we had made it to my car. I said goodbye to Juan, told him I'd see him tomorrow, and got in the car.

Ten minutes later, I found myself wishing Juan had been able to escort me all the way home. Because when I got there, Nolan was waiting for me.

CHAPTER 2

Kaia

I SHOULD HAVE BEEN PAYING ATTENTION.

How did I not know?

No sooner had I slipped the key inside my door, unlocked it, walked in, and flipped on the light when I felt something strange in the air. I didn't understand it, but it was that same odd feeling I'd get if I started thinking I forgot to do something.

Unable to remember anything I could have overlooked, I just assumed it was the result of a rough night the night before followed by a long day today. I'd been up for hours and needed to get some sleep.

Making my way through the apartment to the kitchen, I dumped my things on the counter before grabbing myself some water.

Shower and sleep.

That was what I needed because this would be a long weekend now that I'd decided to pick up an extra night and cover Mateo tomorrow night. Technically, I guess I would be covering him later tonight, considering it was nearly three in the morning.

Yeah, I seriously needed to get some sleep.

But the moment I turned around, prepared to head toward the bathroom to grab a quick shower, I let out a scream.

He was here.

Nolan was standing there, just a few feet away from me.

I was stunned, shocked, and frozen to the spot.

And him?

He acted like nothing was wrong.

"Hey, honey," he said. "How was work tonight?"

My eyes widened in disbelief.

Honey?

Was he serious? He couldn't be serious.

"What are you doing here?" I seethed.

I would have asked how he got into my apartment, but I already knew the answer to that. I stupidly gave him a key a couple of months ago when I had been hoping to see him here waiting for me when I came home from work. Back when I thought he was a decent man. Back when I thought I loved him.

What had I been thinking?

I gave him a key.

And then I didn't remember to get it back after things ended yesterday. That alone led to a whole slew of questions, the most obvious being the question of why he was here and calling me honey when we were no longer together.

Questions aside, it suddenly made sense what that feeling was when I walked through the front door. I had forgotten to do something. After Nolan had taken his hands to me yesterday and walked out, I just assumed it was over between us. It never even crossed my mind that he still had a key to the place.

Nolan took two steps toward me, but I backed away. There was no way I would allow him to come any closer, especially not when I couldn't read him. This made no sense.

When Nolan didn't answer, I demanded, "Tell me why you're here."

"You were away for two weeks, Kaia," he declared, sharing information I already knew. "Is it wrong for me to want to spend time with you after all of that time apart?"

"We're over," I told him, unsure why this wasn't obvious to him.

Shooting me a look of disbelief, one that indicated he believed I was joking, Nolan replied, "We're not over. We didn't agree to that."

My eyes opened so wide; it was a wonder they didn't fall out of my head. "I don't care about agreeing on it or not. We were over the minute you put your hands on me because I decided to spend a few extra days in Wyoming with my sister," I retorted.

"I missed you," he tried to reason. "And it was just like you didn't even care you left me here alone when you decided to stay."

"My sister had a baby," I reminded him. "My new niece arrived. I don't even know why that needs to be stated. If you can't understand why I would want to be there for them, it's clear that after all this time that you don't even know me."

"What about me?" he whined.

Yes, whined. Because what else could I call it? He was throwing a tantrum because he didn't get his way.

"What about you?" I shot back. "You're a grown man. You're completely capable of taking care of yourself. And if you missed me so much and cared about me at all, you would have hauled your ass out to Wyoming *with* me!"

"I had to work," he argued.

"Yeah? And did you see me giving you a bunch of grief about the fact that you chose to do that instead of joining me on a trip for one of the most incredible experiences of my life?" I challenged him. Before he could respond, I answered for him. "No, you didn't. And you know why? Because I'm a big girl, Nolan. I understand that the world doesn't revolve around me. But more than that, I don't need to beg anyone to follow me somewhere they don't want to be. If you wanted to be there with me, you would have been there."

There was a moment of silence as he took in my words. Then, his voice got quiet, and he repeated, "I missed you."

"Not enough," I snapped. "I can think of a million ways you could have proven to me how much you missed me, Nolan. And yet, you didn't choose any of them. You decided to get all bent out of shape when I showed you a new photo Parker sent me of Wren."

"You already showed me like a thousand photos the first night you were back. It's not like the baby looks any different a day or two later," he reasoned.

"So, let me get this straight," I started. "The woman you claim to have missed so much comes back after being gone for two weeks to visit the only family she has and is over the moon about the birth of her new niece, and all you can do is begrudge her the joy of sharing it with you? You can't be bothered to share in that joy and feel it with her?"

"It's like all you care about is your sister and her new baby," he said.

What did I ever see in this man?

This was hopeless. They were my family, and he couldn't get past his selfishness.

Realizing this was a waste of my time, I decided I needed to end this conversation. I'd already wasted nearly a year on this man. I refused to do it any longer.

"Get out," I ordered.

"Kaia—" he said before I cut him off.

"I don't want to hear another thing you have to say," I told him. "Just get out."

Separating his feet just a touch, Nolan crossed his arms over his chest. "I'm not going anywhere," he informed me. "We're not finished."

"We are finished," I insisted. "In every way that we can be. It's over. It's done. You need to leave."

"I already told you I'm not leaving."

My eyes slid to the side, landing on my purse, where I knew I'd find my phone. Unfortunately, Nolan noticed, deduced what I had planned to do, and took another step toward me. I backed up two more steps, belatedly realizing there was nowhere left to retreat to, considering my back was now up against the stove.

Could I hop the counter?

I wasn't sure if I was that nimble, but I knew I had to try.

Like a flash, I launched my body to the side and hurled myself onto the counter. My chest barely connected with the counter when I felt Nolan's hands on me. One yanked back on my hair while the other grasped a fistful of my shirt at the middle of my spine.

He spun me around and laughed in my face. "Where do you think you're going?" he asked, his body bent slightly over mine, which was positioned awkwardly against the countertop.

"Get out," I demanded through clenched teeth.

I continued to struggle against his hold.

"I'll leave when I'm ready," he declared.

He loosened his grip just enough for me to press my palms against his chest and shove him. I managed to get myself fully upright and was about to launch myself toward my purse when Nolan grabbed ahold of me again and slammed me against the refrigerator. He stepped forward, pinning me to the fridge with his body.

This couldn't happen again.

I had to fight back. But my arms were trapped against my chest as he pressed in deeper. I just didn't have the strength to push his body, which was much larger than my own, away from mine.

"Get off of me," I yelled.

As much as I didn't want to be the neighbor in the building who brought this kind of mess to everyone else who lived here, I was hoping somebody would hear me and call the police. I knew that was the only way they'd ever do something. It was the only way the authorities would be forced to do something. Experience had taught me that people like Nolan—people like my father—were never held accountable for their actions. Unless, of course, they were caught in the act. Maybe then I'd have a fighting chance at seeking justice.

And the strange thing about it was that I didn't necessarily care about justice at this point. Sure, I didn't want him to move on and do this to another woman, but deep down, I just wanted him out of my life.

When Nolan didn't move, I decided to risk having all my neighbors hate me and use the only thing I had left.

My voice.

I screamed.

Loud and long.

I didn't care. I yelled for help because that's all I could do.

And that was my mistake.

Because Nolan quickly figured out my tactic and did what he had to do to shut me up. Almost instantly, he pressed his palm flat against my chest to hold me in place as he stepped away and raised his hand. Then he backhanded me across the face.

I was stunned into silence as I tried to regain my composure. The strike had hit with such force; it knocked me completely off balance. Though, when I realized Nolan's hands were no longer on me, I stood up and prepared to make a run for it.

But he was faster than I was.

His fingers curled around my wrist. I began screaming again as I tried to yank my hand away, using all of my body weight to pull back against him. Anything I could do to get away from him, anything to make it harder for him.

That earned me another strike against the cheek. This one was much worse; this one was the one that sent me flying.

I landed back on the kitchen floor with a loud crash. Then I was suffocating. Or, it felt like I was suffocating.

Because Nolan had rolled me to my back and straddled himself over my body. His knees were pressed tightly against my arms, which were stuck at my sides. I couldn't claw his eyes out like I wanted to.

Legs.

I had legs.

I started kicking them as frantically as I could as I began screaming again.

"Shut up," Nolan asserted.

"Never," I shouted. "I'll never do another damn thing for you. Help!!!"

In the next moment, I wondered if I'd made the smartest choice. Because Nolan brought one hand down to cover my mouth and my nose as the other went to my throat. And he wasn't gentle about it.

Mere seconds felt like an eternity as I fought to calm myself down. I needed air. I needed to breathe.

Just before I thought I'd pass out, there were several loud raps at the door. Nolan froze, though his grip around my neck loosened. Hope surged inside me.

Hope and relief.

Someone heard me.

I heard several more knocks before a voice called out, "Kaia? Is everything okay?"

Clara. My neighbor. My neighbor who had two small children.

Oh, God.

I didn't know what to do. Though, it wasn't like I could do anything because Nolan still had me pinned to the floor.

Please call the police. Please call the police.

Clara knocked again. "Kaia? I heard yelling. Should I call for help?"

Yes! Please!

"Everything is okay," Nolan returned, raising his voice so she could hear. "We were moving furniture around."

"At this hour?" Clara returned suspiciously. "It's the middle of the night. Is that true, Kaia? Are you sure you're okay?"

"Fucking nosy bitch," he quietly hissed.

Nolan narrowed his eyes on me. Then, keeping his hand over my mouth, he removed his hand entirely from my throat and reached up to the counter.

"Kaia?" Clara called again. "I think I'm going to call the police, just to be sure you're alright."

I always knew I liked Clara. I would have to buy her a bouquet of flowers or babysit her kids so she could take a day to go to the spa or something. That was, of course, assuming I got through this alive.

Survive. That was what I needed to focus my attention on just then because I saw something shiny flash in my line of vision before I felt the tip of the blade at my throat. Nolan had gotten a knife.

Terror.

All I felt was terror.

And shame. And disgust.

How did I ever manage to love and care for this person? Referring to him as a person was difficult enough. I couldn't call him a man. He wasn't anything close to resembling what a man was supposed to be. And I knew good men existed; my sister found one of the best.

At the thought of Parker, I squeezed my eyes shut tight. Visions of my beautiful niece, my sister, and my brother-in-law danced in my head.

Please don't let me die like this.

I was pulled from my thoughts when Nolan quietly demanded, "Look at me."

My eyes shot open.

"Tell her you are fine," he whispered. "Say one stupid thing, and my hand might slip on this knife."

Tears leaked from the corners of my eyes and slid back into my hair. I would do anything, anything to survive. I would do whatever I had to do to make sure my sister wouldn't have to come and identify my body.

Oh, God.

Parker.

Clara's voice penetrated the tense silence one last time. "Kaia?" she called impatiently.

"Do you hear me?" Nolan asked, his voice hushed and tense.

Since his hand was still covering my mouth, I lifted my head slightly to indicate I understood.

With the knife still pressed against my throat, Nolan slowly peeled his fingers away from my mouth.

"I'm—" I stopped to clear my throat. "I'm okay, Clara. Sorry if we woke you."

"Are you sure you're alright?"

For half a second, I considered screaming and telling her to call the police, but Nolan gave me a warning look as I felt the tip of the knife pierce my skin.

"I'm sure," I called back.

There was a moment of hesitation. "O… Okay," she returned. Even in my panicked state, I could hear the uncertainty and doubt in her voice. I just hoped it was enough to push her to call the police anyway.

For the next several seconds, Nolan didn't move. It wasn't

until we heard a door close outside my apartment, indicating Clara had gone back to her place, that he spoke.

"You're lucky," he said, the knife still at my throat. "I don't trust that woman, so I'm leaving. But if you think this is over, think again. And if I so much as get a whiff of you going to the police about this, I will make it my mission to destroy your life. You'll never work at another club in this town again."

Oh no. He wasn't going to take that away from me. I wanted to kick him in the balls right then, but since he was still sitting on top of me, I couldn't. Plus, I still didn't want to die.

So, I assured him, "I won't tell them."

"You won't like what happens if you do," he promised.

The next thing I knew, he got up, set the knife on the counter, and look down at me. "We're not done."

Then he turned and walked away.

I stayed frozen to the spot. And when I heard my front door open and close not even thirty seconds later, I sprang up to my feet, ran to my bedroom, and packed a bag. Twenty-five minutes later, I checked into a hotel.

And when I was tucked safely under the covers, I curled up on my side, reached out for my phone, and looked at a picture Parker sent me not even twelve hours earlier. It was her and Wren. Wren had her eyes open wide, and she was laughing. Parker was ecstatic that she caught Wren smiling.

That was when I burst into tears.

CHAPTER 3

Kaia

As I stood in the bathroom of my hotel room, I started to wonder if the lighting was just that good or if my face just looked that bad.

It was early Friday evening, and even though I had gone out earlier in the day, I ultimately decided to come back here to get myself ready for work.

Surprisingly, I slept well last night. I wasn't sure if it was simply the fact that I was exhausted or if it was my body and mind giving me the break I needed from my new reality. Maybe it was a combination of both.

Either way, I was grateful.

Because the moment I opened my eyes, everything that happened last night hit me like a ton of bricks. I could have died.

While I felt fortunate to have made it through the altercation with Nolan alive, I still ended up with plenty of muscle aches, soreness, and bruising on my neck and face.

I knew I needed to go back to my place at some point,

but there was no way I'd even consider it so long as I knew that Nolan had a key and could come and go as he pleased. So, after giving myself some time this morning to soak my body in the bathtub, I got myself dressed, took photos of what Nolan had done to me, put on a bit of makeup, and left for a couple of hours.

On the walk to my car, I made a call to my landlord and wasn't surprised that I got his voicemail and needed to leave a message.

"Hey, Rudy, it's Kaia Banks," I started. "I wanted to call and give you a heads-up that I am heading out this morning to get new locks for the doors on my apartment. I… I lost my spare key, and I'm worried that it might have ended up in the wrong hands, so I figured it was best to be on the safe side and just change the locks. I hope that's okay. Please give me a call back if you have any issues. Thanks."

No sooner had I pulled into the parking lot at the hardware store when I got a return call from Rudy.

"Hello?" I answered.

"Hey, Kaia. I just got your message about wanting to change the locks," he said.

"Yeah, um, I feel so stupid for losing that spare key," I began. "I just think it's better to be cautious, so I wanted to change them. You don't mind, do you?" I asked.

"Not at all," he assured me. "Do you need any help with them? My maintenance guys are tied up today, but I might have some time this afternoon. I could stop over and get them changed for you."

That was nice of him, and in any other case, I probably would have taken him up on his offer. But I wanted to do this on my own.

"I appreciate the offer, Rudy," I replied. "But I think I can handle it. I'm already out at the hardware store anyway. I'll be sure to get something that matches as closely to what's there right now."

"Do whatever you've got to do," Rudy urged. "And if you change your mind and want or need the help, just give me a call."

"Will do. Thank you so much."

"You're welcome, Kaia. Take care."

With Rudy's approval, I wasted not a second more. I dashed into the hardware store, picked up a new lockset and tools, and made my way back to my apartment.

I felt a bit of anxiety as I opened my door and walked inside. Fortunately, it did not seem as though Nolan had returned after he left last night. After doing a quick scan of the space and noting that everything was just as I'd left it last night, I got to work on changing the lock.

Before I knew it, I had gotten everything changed and was on my way back to the hotel. Best of all, I hadn't run into Clara while I was there. I knew I'd be confronted by that situation at some point, but it hadn't even been a full twenty-four hours yet. I wasn't ready to deal with it, though.

I'd already felt bad enough that I'd stretched the truth a bit when I called Rudy. I didn't want to have to continue going around lying to everyone. That said, considering Clara had two young children, I didn't want her to think there was any reason to be alarmed or concerned about where she was living.

Truthfully, there were no really bad parts of town in Poppy Valley. In my experience, it never was about the place someone lived anyway. It was about the people. And sometimes, people made bad choices. Nolan made a horrible choice, but I wholeheartedly believed there was no reason for Clara to be worried.

So, until I figured out how to best deal with what happened the night before, I thanked my lucky stars, which I would have appreciated more if they'd been around last night, that I was able to get the locks changed before I ran into her.

I knew if she'd seen me, I would have had no choice but to tell her the truth, mostly because it would have been hard to hide the fact that I looked like this.

Even with makeup, I was struggling to hide the evidence of what Nolan did to me. I knew that was the case when I went to the hardware store and received a couple of odd looks; some were concerned, and others were curious.

I avoided them.

Just like I was hoping to be able to do tonight when I got to work. The one thing I'd have going for me would be the dim lighting. I thought it would be enough, but I couldn't be sure. For that reason, I took just a little bit of extra time to get everything covered up.

And while I took the time to do that, a million thoughts ran through my mind. I was torn between feeling relieved that I was alive after what happened but also ashamed of what I'd allowed to happen.

What did it say about the kind of woman I was that I didn't run to the police last night? I should have. I knew I should have.

Two things stopped me, though.

Just as it had flitted through my mind last night amid the chaos, I couldn't ignore the fact that nothing was ever done to help Parker and me when we were kids. Our father had always been careful about how he struck us. Parker took the brunt of the abuse, continually stepping in and sacrificing herself for me. She did an excellent job of covering up any marks he left because in the one instance that a teacher had started to dig a little deeper, nothing ever came of it. Well, nothing but a bit more fear for us. Parker and I knew that if the right people got involved, we could be removed from our father's house. But if that happened, it was possible we could be taken away and separated from one another. That was never an option for us.

But the other reason that I didn't go to the police was that I just wanted a bit more time to figure things out. It made me uneasy to recall Nolan's words to me last night.

We're not done.

I shuddered just remembering the promise I heard in his tone. It sent chills down my spine in the most horrible way. And that should have sent me running to the police. But I trusted that he would follow through on his threat to destroy my career if he had any indication I had gone to the authorities.

Nolan had the connections and the power in this small town, and I was convinced he wouldn't hesitate to use either of them if he felt it was necessary.

For the time being, I was going to stay at the hotel. I needed time to figure out how to handle this situation and keep myself protected. And if I was at my place, I had a feeling I'd be constantly worried about him coming back. Changing the locks would only do so much to keep him out. If he was determined enough, the addition of new locks wasn't going to stop him.

After taking one last look at myself in the mirror, deciding I'd done the best I could, I turned off the light and walked out of the bathroom. Once I'd gathered up everything I'd need for my night at work, I grabbed my room key and walked out.

Twenty minutes later, I made a beeline across the main space at Club Infinity to my booth. All I wanted to do was get inside without being seen. Of course, not wanting to make it seem so obvious that I was avoiding everyone, I lifted a hand toward the bar and waved as I passed by. It was dark enough, and I turned my head so quickly, I was sure nobody really thought twice about it.

But my mistake was not remembering who I'd run into when I made it to the booth.

Juan.

Shit.

He was standing there, talking with another member of the security staff. It wasn't uncommon to see that, and I was grateful he was distracted.

I'd keep my head down and use my hair to shield my face from them. It wasn't completely dark in the club yet, and I thought I'd done a decent job with my makeup, so I prayed I'd get lucky.

Maybe I'd already suffered enough, perhaps it was my lucky day, but I let out a sigh of relief when I made it inside the booth without needing to interact directly with anyone.

But it was no more than three or four minutes later when there was a knock on the door that led into the booth. I looked up and saw Juan's face in the window.

Juan opened the door and stepped inside.

"Hey, Banks," he greeted me.

"Hi, Juan," I returned, keeping my head down as I fumbled with my equipment in front of me.

"Listen, I just wanted to let you know that Zach is going

to be standing guard out here by you tonight," he started. "He's the newest member on the team. I just wanted to make sure you were aware of it beforehand. I'll bring him over to introduce you when he gets here."

"Okay, sure," I responded, still not looking up at him. "Thanks for letting me know."

Silence filled the room, and when I glanced out of the corner of my eye, I could see that Juan had made no effort to walk out of the booth. I was about to ask if he needed something else when he called my name.

I let out a sigh of relief, returned my attention to my work, and responded, "Yeah?"

"Everything okay?" he asked.

"Yeah," I quickly replied.

"Is there a reason you're avoiding looking at me?" he pressed.

Nope. It wasn't my lucky day.

Slowly, I lifted my gaze to Juan's. His eyes narrowed on my face, surprise washed over him, and he asked, "What happened?"

Tears instantly filled my eyes.

Shit.

I did not want to cry.

I shook my head, hoping he would understand I didn't want to talk about it.

"That's why there's no longer a man, isn't it? He put his hands on you. How did I not see it last night?" he questioned me.

Shaking my head again, feeling the tightness in my throat, I rasped, "It... it happened last night after I got home. Please, Juan, I don't want to talk about this."

His eyes widened. "So, he did it," he declared. "I was just guessing. Please tell me you got checked out and went to the police."

"No, I didn't," I confessed. "And I don't want them involved."

"Why not?"

"I just don't," I insisted. "Please, Juan. Please let this go."

Now it was Juan's turn to shake his head. "I can't do that, Banks."

There was a knock on the door, and my body instantly tensed. Juan noticed, turned, and blocked me from the view of whoever was behind the door.

"Hey, Juan, sorry to interrupt. Tyler told me you wanted to see me," the unfamiliar voice said.

"Yeah, um, sorry," Juan said. "I was going to have you working here tonight, Zach, but I'm going to have you somewhere else instead. Give me a couple of minutes, and I'll be right out."

"Sure."

When Juan turned to face me again, I said, "Zach isn't going to be working here tonight?"

"Until I know what happened and that you're not in any danger, I'm covering your back," Juan answered.

If nothing else, I appreciate Juan's protectiveness. Even though I knew he wouldn't have anyone on his team he didn't trust, it warmed my heart to know he wanted to be the one responsible for keeping me safe.

Of course, I didn't think Nolan would be stupid enough to come here and try anything. Then again, I didn't know he was an abusive asshole either, so anything was possible.

"Thank you," I rasped, feeling my emotions get the best of me.

Juan held out his hand and urged, "Come here, Banks."

I knew if I allowed him to hug me, I'd cry, but I was in some serious need of comfort. So, I stepped forward into his big body, felt his arms come around me, and let the tears leak from my eyes.

Following a beat of silence, Juan asked, "How long has this been going on?"

I pressed my cheek against Juan's chest and answered, "Twice. I thought he understood we were done after the first time two nights ago. He was waiting at my apartment when I got home last night."

"I'm following you home tonight," he insisted. "I'll go inside and check it out for you."

Pulling my face from his chest, I looked up at him and shared, "I'm staying at a hotel. I changed my lock at my apartment today, but I just want another night to think about what I'm going to do."

"Then, I'll see you safely to your hotel," he said. "And if you're not going to take this to the police, which I think is a terrible idea and would urge you to reconsider, we need to make sure you can keep yourself safe."

I took half a step back, and Juan loosened his hold on me. "It's okay," I assured him. "I appreciate what you're offering, but you don't need to get involved in this mess."

"I'm already in it," he stated. "I'll let you get back to doing your thing in here. I've got you covered. And later, we'll talk about what you're going to do to keep yourself safe."

Realizing I wasn't going to talk him out of it, I decided not to argue with him. "Thanks, Juan."

"Anytime, Banks."

With that, he opened the door and stepped out of the booth. I gave myself a moment to let the conversation I'd just had with Juan run through my mind. Then, I took in a deep breath, let it out, and got myself ready for the night ahead.

If nothing else, I knew work would offer the perfect distraction. And the music would definitely help improve my mood.

Sure enough, within an hour, I was feeling much better.

Throughout the night, I glanced over at Juan and saw him looking a little tense. He was generally always very serious given the nature of his job, but it wasn't hard to see that what he learned tonight was doing a number on him.

I hated that.

By the end of the night, I saw just a smidgen of the tension leave him. It wasn't everything I had hoped for, but it was better than nothing.

"Ready?" he asked when I walked out of my booth.

I nodded. "Yeah."

"Do you need to stop at home for anything?" he questioned me as we walked toward the exit.

"No, I got a couple of things earlier today," I told him.

He indicated his understanding with a chin lift and opened the door. Twenty minutes later, despite my insistence that he didn't need to follow me there, Juan was walking me into the hotel and seeing me safely up to my room.

Once he confirmed my room was secure, he moved to the door to leave and stopped there.

"Is everything okay?" I asked.

He sighed. "I wish this weren't necessary, but given your decision not to take this to the police, I don't think there's any other option," he started. I watched as he dug his hand into his pocket and pulled out a business card. He held it out to me and demanded, "You need to call these guys. They trained me. They trained everyone on my team. And I'm confident they'll see to it that you can do what you need to do to defend yourself."

I took the card from Juan and responded, "Thank you."

"Don't wait," he urged. "Go there immediately. Tomorrow morning if you can."

"Okay," I replied.

"Promise me."

"What?" I asked.

"Promise me that you're going to do this," he clarified.

Wow. This was affecting him more than I thought it was.

"I promise."

With that and a downward jerk of his head, Juan opened the door and stepped out. "You need anything between now and then—you need anything at all—you have my number," he said.

My brows pulled together. "No, I don't," I remarked.

He jerked his head in the direction of the card he'd handed me. "It's on the back of that card. Don't be afraid to use it, Banks," he ordered.

I offered a friendly smile and gave him a nod.

A moment later, I was standing alone in my hotel room, feeling grateful I had a friend like Juan.

Then I looked down at the card in my hand.

Archer Tactical.

I guess I knew what I was going to be doing tomorrow morning.

CHAPTER 4

Remi

"**T**HANKS, AGAIN, FOR SUCH A GREAT CLASS, REMI. I really learned a lot this week."

"You're welcome, Courtney," I replied. "I'm happy to hear you say you're benefiting from the classes. That's the goal. Confidence, right?"

Courtney smiled at me and nodded. "Right."

She hesitated a moment before she turned and walked out of the training room. I stayed behind to gather up a few things while the rest of the class filed out.

It had been a great class.

As part owner of Archer Tactical, the premier self-defense and tactical firearm training company, it was always nice to know that professionals and civilians alike were benefiting from the instruction we provided.

It was Monday evening, and I'd just finished up my final class of the day. I generally looked forward to the beginning of the workweek. I know a lot of people hated Mondays, but I didn't. It was always a chance to start fresh and learn something new. Then again, I tended to look at every day that same way—Monday or otherwise.

Ten minutes after my class had ended and the last of the attendees had walked out, I finished cleaning up in the training room and made my way out front. It was nearly closing time.

Much to my surprise, I found my younger brothers, Vaughn and Deacon, were back. They were at the front of the facility in the space we referred to as the showroom. Our building was large, most of it comprised of individual training rooms, but we also had an indoor and outdoor shooting range. In addition, we had another building that we used to set up mock drills for advanced training for law enforcement and members of the military who wanted to hone their skills.

We didn't sell firearms, but we offered lots of accessories ranging from holsters and ammo to protective training gear. All of that could be purchased in our showroom, where I currently found my brothers.

Vaughn was seated at one of the stools behind the counter, and Deacon was standing off to the side of it, leaning his forearms on the countertop.

"Hey, guys, how'd it go today?" I asked.

Deacon, the youngest of us, answered, "It was awesome. We worked with a really talented group of guys today."

"Yeah, and they were motivated like I can't recall ever seeing before with another group," Vaughn added. "It wasn't necessarily that they were more qualified than anyone else, but they had a passion for learning that I don't think I've ever seen."

"That's fantastic news," I said. "It should be a good week then, right?"

"Yep," Deacon replied.

Deacon and Vaughn were leading a SWAT team training course this week. It was something we regularly did. This was what the professional training we did was all about.

Sometimes, we held introductory and beginner classes for self-defense and handgun training. We also had intermediate-level training that students could advance to when they completed our introductory courses and wanted more efficiency in their defensive strategies. And finally, we offered advanced classes for tactical training in combat situations. This was where most of the professionals fit in.

I wasn't surprised that my brothers were excited about the work they had ahead of them this week. It was always a thrilling experience to know we were doing our part to help members of law enforcement to prepare for the worst of situations. And there was something about working in the field—literally—that added that extra layer of eagerness.

"I think I'm going to need to get in on the next one," I said.

Vaughn let out a laugh. "What? You didn't enjoy your training today?" he joked.

I knew what he was trying to do, but it wasn't going to work. "Training was fantastic today," I assured him. "I'm just saying that it'd be nice to get out in the field for training since I've been handling so much of the indoor training lately."

"Bro, you spent the evening with a bunch of women," Deacon reminded me. "I wouldn't be complaining."

I rolled my eyes. "I'm not complaining," I insisted. "And don't say it like that. Those women are here to learn self-defense, not find their next hookup."

That was the truth. Every Monday evening and every other Saturday, we offered women's self-defense and empowerment classes. Over the years, we found that many women were interested in learning self-defense techniques, but several of them were too intimidated to join classes with men. A male instructor was one thing. Beyond that, it was too much.

"Is that what you're searching for, Remi? A hookup?" Vaughn asked.

I shook my head. "No. And you know what I mean," I returned, narrowing my eyes on him.

"Are you telling me none of the women here tonight were cute?" Deacon asked.

I sighed. "That doesn't matter. I'm a professional, and that's what these women are here looking for," I told him. "They don't want to come here feeling like they've got to be on the defensive about anything other than their training."

Vaughn's eyes slid to Deacon's, and his brows shot up. Deacon chuckled.

"What's that about?" I asked.

"I don't know… we think you might be mistaken," Vaughn advised.

Confusion washed over me. My brothers and I would often tease one another about finding a woman and settling down. It was just the way it was. But it didn't leak into us ever considering doing something unprofessional when it came to the business we ran together.

Realizing I had no idea what he was getting at, Deacon explained, "Courtney lingered."

"What?"

"Courtney," he repeated. "Vaughn and I were already out here when your class let out. To say she lingered a bit would be an understatement."

"Her eyes kept going back in the direction of the training room," Vaughn added. "There's no doubt she was considering walking back to talk to you about something that had nothing to do with self-defense."

"How have you not noticed this?" Deacon pressed.

I had noticed. It wasn't difficult to see that Courtney was attracted to me. I wasn't being conceited about it. She just didn't hide it very well. The thing was, as sweet as she was, Courtney just wasn't my type.

I held my hands up in front of me. "Guys, relax," I said. "I have, but I'm not going there."

"She's cute," Vaughn noted.

"And she's into you in a tremendous way, Rem," Deacon added. "If a woman looked at me the way Courtney looks at you, I don't know that I'd risk letting her get away."

I sat on one of the stools and sighed. "I feel bad," I started. "She's a sweetheart, and she is pretty. But I'm not into her like that."

"She's sweet, pretty, and into you," Vaughn said. "What else could you want?"

"What else could you need?" Deacon wondered.

I looked away. "Spark, ambition, confidence, and a connection," I answered. "Even though I know the ambition will come with the confidence as she continues to train, there still isn't a spark there. And I think it's because I know she'd be the kind of woman who would bow to my every whim. She could grow to become a force in a high-pressure situation, but that would only be when she needed to fight someone to protect herself. I'm not a threat, so she'd never challenge me."

"You make a valid point," Vaughn remarked.

"Maybe she's just nervous," Deacon suggested.

"Of course she is," I confirmed.

"So why don't you make it easy on her and yourself by cutting to the chase and asking her out? She wouldn't say no," my brother informed me.

"Deacon, that would be wrong on so many levels, and you know it. I'm not going to do that to her," I insisted.

Deacon grunted, and I wanted to laugh. He might have acted tough, but the truth was that he'd never do something like that either. If he wasn't seriously into a woman, he wouldn't ever try to take advantage of an attraction a woman had to him. Vaughn wouldn't either.

Part of that had a lot to do with who our parents raised us to be, and part of it had to do with the fact that we had a younger sister we'd never want to see treated that way, but most of it had to do with the fact that it just wasn't right.

So, Deacon might have acted frustrated, but I knew he was anything but.

"Alright, so, then we need to do something about this," Deacon declared.

"About what?" Vaughn asked.

Deacon's eyes shifted to our brother's before he clarified, "The fact that we're all in our thirties and still single."

I laughed. Now, Deacon's frustration made sense. I was thirty-five, Vaughn was thirty-three, and Deacon was thirty-one.

Following a brief stretch of silence, Vaughn noted, "Can you believe Monroe's been married for years now, and we're all still waiting for the right one to come along?"

"And to think we thought she needed our help when it came to finding someone," Deacon muttered.

Truer words had never been spoken. Monroe was a

determined woman. She knew what she wanted, and she went after it. Literally. And now, our sister was happily married with a handful of kids. She was the happiest we'd ever seen her, and we were all thrilled that she'd found and got exactly what she deserved in her life.

But what my brothers were saying had me pausing to think. I was thirty-five now, and I wasn't getting any younger. I wanted what my sister had found. I wanted a wife and children. And when I allowed myself to think about it, I started to wonder if it was ever going to happen. Maybe I was being too picky.

"So what do you suggest?" I asked, resolving myself to the fact that maybe we needed to put a bit more effort into it, the same way Monroe had.

"We go out," Deacon declared. "Next Saturday night since Vaughn and I will be finishing up the final portion of that SWAT training this Saturday. That's a long day, and it's always killer. I'm not sure I'll be up for heading out that night."

"Out?" I repeated.

"Yeah. Almost two weeks from now. But we'll go somewhere nice," he insisted.

I wasn't exactly sure that I'd encounter the woman I wanted by spending a night out; I always thought I'd find her here. Maybe that was strange, but I had this idea that some beautiful and determined woman was going to walk through the front door of Archer Tactical, and everything would suddenly make sense. But since that hadn't happened, I had no choice but to agree. At this point, I didn't have anything to lose by spending a night out with my brothers.

"Okay," I agreed. "I'm in."

"Me too," Vaughn said.

Just then, the front door opened, and something seized in my chest.

The only people left in the building were my brothers and me, which was a good thing. Because if not, students and employees alike would have seen me struggling to remain in control for what felt like the first time in my life.

The most beautiful woman I'd ever seen walked through the door and was making her way toward us. From a distance, I could see her shoulder-length hair that hung in loose waves in a color that could only be described as golden. Her body was petite and fit, her legs toned and slender. She had a trim waist and breasts that were the perfect size to fit inside my hands.

She had all of that, and it still wasn't the best thing about her. What I liked the most about her was her confidence. Yes, confidence. There was no denying she had it. Because she was walking toward my brothers and me. And the way she was doing it, approaching three men, with a determined look in her eye, it was clear this woman was on a mission. She wasn't about to let anyone get in her way.

Fuck, she was beautiful.

When she stopped in front of us, by some miracle, I managed to find my voice.

"Hi," I greeted her.

"Hi," she returned.

I felt that one word shoot straight to my dick.

"If you're here for the women's self-defense class, you just missed it," Deacon jumped in.

Her stunning hazel eyes left mine for the first time since she walked in and moved to Vaughn before they finally settled on Deacon. "I didn't know there was a self-defense class," she shared. "That's not why I'm here."

Not wanting her to look at either of my brothers, I asked, "So, how can I help you?"

"I was given your card by a friend who said you offered self-defense training," she started. "I was wondering if I could sign up."

"Sure," I answered, thinking that I no longer cared that Deacon and Vaughn were working out in the field this week. I'd be happy to stay in for the next five months if I was going to get to see this woman and train with her. "We offer women's self-defense and empowerment classes every Monday night and every other Saturday morning. This coming Saturday will be the week we're on."

She blinked in surprise, and something that looked a bit like disappointment washed over her face. Maybe our schedule wasn't going to work with hers.

"Oh," she replied. I could see her mind working. A moment later, she asked, "So, you don't offer private lessons?"

Private lessons weren't something we typically did simply because our classes were full in the evenings. Offering private lessons for one-on-one instruction would require more staffing. And given the nature of what we did, there was no way we could hire just anybody looking for a job.

Instead of answering her question, I countered, "Do our class times not work with your schedule?"

Shaking her head, she insisted, "It's not that. I work odd nights, and sometimes, Mondays are one of them. It's just that… well, I was hoping for something more. I thought perhaps you offered morning sessions as well."

"I could do that for you," I told her.

Out of the corner of my eye, I vaguely noticed Vaughn and Deacon leaning forward at my declaration. There was no doubt they knew precisely what was going through my mind. I didn't ever volunteer to do one-on-one sessions unless there were unique circumstances. But for this woman, I would.

"Oh, okay. That's great news. When can I start?" she asked.

"Does tomorrow morning work?"

She nodded. "Yeah, that would be excellent."

I extended my hand to her and said, "I'm Remi. I'll be your instructor."

She lifted her hand, pressed her palm to mine, and shook my hand. "I'm Kaia. I'll be your student."

Gorgeous. Determined. And funny.

Yep.

I liked where this was going.

When Kaia pulled her hand away, I asked, "What time can you get here?"

"What time do you want me?"

Now, I thought.

"Can you make it here by ten o'clock?"

"I can," she confirmed. Following a brief pause, she asked, "Do I have to fill out any paperwork? And how much are classes going to cost?"

I didn't want to charge this woman anything. Glancing over at my brothers for a brief second, it was clear they knew exactly what I was thinking. I returned my attention to Kaia and replied, "Not now. I can have you complete some formal paperwork tomorrow morning, but your first class is on the house. We'll get a feel for what you're looking to accomplish, how often you want to train, and we'll go from there."

"Really?"

"Yep."

"That's awesome. Thank you," she exclaimed. There was an awkward moment of silence before she said, "Well, I should probably get home and get some rest then. I'll see you tomorrow morning. It was nice to meet you, Remi."

"Likewise, Kaia. Have a good night."

She smiled at me and whispered, "You too."

With that, Kaia turned and walked away. I was too stunned to move.

That smile.

That gorgeous smile aimed at me was something I felt somewhere deep in my gut. And that's when I knew I wanted that. I wanted to see that every day for the rest of my life.

While I might not have been able to move, that didn't mean I couldn't see. My eyes followed Kaia as she walked back to the front door.

Suffice it to say, there wasn't a single thing I didn't like about the way she moved.

I couldn't wait until tomorrow.

"Earth to Remi."

I looked to my left and saw both of my brothers wearing amused expressions.

"What?" I asked.

"What happened to being professional?" Vaughn teased.

"I was professional," I insisted.

His brows shot up, but it was Deacon who spoke. "And yet you offered private instruction," he pointed out.

"Yeah. I mean, she was referred to us by a friend," I reminded him. "I think we should do what we can to accommodate referrals, don't you?"

"You can tell yourself that's what it's about all you want. You know that has absolutely *nothing* to do with it," Vaughn maintained.

Shaking my head, I got up and started getting ready to close up for the night. "You're both crazy," I said.

"We didn't even exist for the last five minutes," Deacon noted. "Not for you and not for her."

Yep, I had noticed that. Other than when Deacon spoke after she first walked in, Kaia hadn't looked at him or Vaughn.

I loved it.

"It might just be the two of us next weekend, Deac," Vaughn said. "I get the feeling Remi is going to have other plans."

He wasn't wrong about that. While I couldn't say for sure what would happen, I did know that I had every intention of trying to make plans for every weekend moving forward. Plans that included Kaia.

"If I'm lucky," I replied.

With that, I focused my effort on finishing up my tasks for the night and went home looking forward to what the next day would bring.

CHAPTER 5

Kaia

CHAOTIC.

That was the best way to describe how life had been over the last couple of days.

As it turned out, I didn't immediately take care of what I had promised Juan I would. Though he never gave me a time constraint when he urged me to promise him I'd do something about what had happened, it was clear to see when I walked into work on Saturday night and admitted that I hadn't yet contacted or visited Archer Tactical that Juan was disappointed.

When I woke up that morning, I took a look in the mirror and just couldn't do it. The last thing I wanted to do was walk into a place like that looking the way I did. I mean, maybe that was the whole point. Perhaps they should have seen what I looked like. I couldn't explain it; I just didn't want people seeing me like that. It was bad enough that Juan had already noticed.

Much as I expected, Juan kept himself on duty right

outside my DJ booth on Saturday evening. The night had gone off without a hitch. And once again, Juan escorted me back to the hotel.

"How long are you planning to stay in this hotel?" he asked as we rode the elevator up to my floor.

"I'm going to go home tomorrow," I told him. "I don't have to work, so I can go home in the morning. I have to run a few errands, but then I'll be home the rest of the day. Since I won't be out late, I think I'll be alright staying home."

"If you want, call me before you head back there. I have no problem checking things out for you before you go inside," he offered as the elevator doors opened. He held his hand out, indicating I could step off ahead of him.

"I appreciate that, Juan," I started. "But I don't think he'll try anything in broad daylight. Besides, one of my neighbors is already a little wary since she was woken in the middle of the night Thursday night. She was banging on the door, checking to make sure I was okay."

"Why didn't you tell her you needed help?" he wondered.

"I couldn't," I returned, coming to a stop outside my hotel room. I waved the key card in front of the door handle, heard the lock open, and pushed inside.

Once we stepped inside, Juan checked things out, confirmed it was all good, and pressed, "I don't understand. Why couldn't you tell her to call the police?"

I dropped my gaze to the ground and closed my eyes. After taking in a deep breath as I recalled what happened that night, I opened my eyes, returned them to Juan, and shared, "He had a knife against my throat."

I wasn't sure I'd ever seen such controlled anger before in

my life. Whatever Juan was feeling, he felt it in a way that I could see him going through it, but he never let it out.

Once he'd taken some time to deal with the information I'd just shared, he insisted, "I want you to call me before you head back to your place tomorrow. Not only do I want to make sure it's all good there, but I want to make sure that you're alright. If you haven't really been back there for an extended period since that night, you might find yourself struggling. We can hang for a bit and make sure you're good before I take off again."

My shoulders fell as my head dropped to one side. "You're such a good friend, Juan. Thank you for looking out for me," I rasped.

"Anytime, Banks. You know that."

I nodded and gave him a hug before he took off.

And the next day, after I left the hotel and ran my errands, I gave Juan a call. Truth be told, I wasn't doing it for myself. Something about the way he'd been with me over the previous two nights made me do it. The last thing I wanted was him spending all week worried that I wasn't okay. So, I did it for him.

He met me at my apartment, saw me safely inside, and stayed with me for a little while until he was confident that I wasn't going to lose my mind. Before he left, he reminded me of the promise I made to him.

Then, on Monday, after I finally convinced myself it was time to follow through on my promise, I stepped out of the apartment and ran into Clara.

If nothing else, I was grateful that the evidence of my Thursday night brawl with Nolan was no longer visible when I had makeup on.

Nevertheless, at the sight of me, Clara declared, "Oh, thank goodness. I've been so worried about you, Kaia."

Noting she had both of her young children with her, there was no way I was going to tell her the truth about what happened that night. Instead, I apologized, "I'm so sorry about what happened the other night. I never meant to wake anyone."

Shaking her head as though she were dismissing the thought, she insisted, "Oh, please, don't worry about that. I'm just glad you're okay. I've really been worried about you ever since that night. And I kept telling myself that if I didn't see you or talk to you by the end of the weekend, I was going to do something about it." She let out a massive sigh of relief and continued, "Gosh, I'm so glad you're alright."

Honestly, I started to feel bad. This poor woman had enough to deal with raising two young children on her own. It was nice, though, to know that I had people looking out for me, genuine people who cared.

I reached out, gave her a hug, and insisted, "I'm okay. I'm sorry I worried you. And if there's ever anything I can do to make it up to you, don't hesitate to ask. I'm an aunt now, so I need practice for when I go back to visit my niece again if you ever need someone to watch the kids for a couple hours."

Clara's eyes widened. "That would be incredible. Thank you."

Considering she was the reason Nolan stopped choking me that night, I didn't think she needed to be the one thanking me, but I didn't tell her that. Instead, I replied, "You're welcome. And thank you."

And now, I was pacing my apartment because it was

Tuesday morning. I had to leave in fifteen minutes to meet Remi at Archer Tactical.

Not long after I ran into Clara, I'd taken off to follow through on what I said I was going to do. And walking toward the front door of Archer Tactical felt a lot like a step in the right direction. With each step I took toward the entrance, I felt a strong sense of determination and power.

I was going to do this.

I needed to do this.

I deserved this.

Because I wasn't going to be scared. And I definitely wasn't going to sit around waiting for Nolan to make his next move.

Of course, I never expected to walk in and become overwhelmed by the sight of the man in front of me. He was incredibly handsome. But I refused to be deterred. I was there for a reason.

Fortunately, I managed to solidify this morning's session. At the time, I thought it was a victory. Now, I wasn't so sure.

That wasn't to say that I wasn't excited about this. I was. It was just that I felt some nerves about it, too. And the problem was that I was convinced my nerves had nothing to do with what I was going to be doing today and everything to do with who I'd be doing it with.

I'd have been lying if I said that I didn't feel something intense wash over me the moment he held my hand in his.

No.

No.

I was overreacting. I was sure the reason I felt anything was that Remi had chosen that very moment to tell me that he was the one who'd be my instructor. That was all it was.

It had to be. Once I got there and got started, I was sure everything would be fine.

And even if that didn't happen, it didn't matter. I had to do this because even though Nolan hadn't attempted to contact me since the night he was at my apartment waiting for me when I got home from work, I knew he wasn't finished. I knew he'd be back.

I just needed to make sure that by the time he was ready to approach me again, I'd be prepared for him. As much as I would have loved to move completely, that simply wasn't an option for me. So, I had to do what I had to do to protect myself.

Nobody else was going to do it for me.

On that thought, I stopped pacing, grabbed my purse, my phone, and my keys, and took off.

When I pulled into the lot, I saw only a handful of cars in the parking lot. I had a feeling most of the people who would be coming to a place like this for any kind of training worked regular business hours and probably attended evening classes. I took that to mean good things for me because I wouldn't have to worry about anyone seeing me flailing. I wasn't sure how good I'd be at this.

The next thing I knew, I was walking through the entrance again.

And the moment I did, my eyes instantly connected with Remi's. He waved, smiled, and greeted me.

"Good morning, Kaia," he said.

I came to a stop in front of him and returned, "Good morning, Remi."

"Are you ready to get started?" he asked.

"I think so," I answered. "Do you have forms for me to complete?"

At my question, Remi's expression changed. "Let's have you just sign the waiver," he said. "We'll figure everything else out after we go through your first session."

"Okay."

I quickly signed the waiver and followed Remi through an open door. Once we were inside, he closed the door behind us and moved toward the far side of the room where a couple of chairs were located.

"Grab a seat," he urged.

Sit down?

"Aren't we going to work on self-defense?" I asked.

"We are. But first, we need to talk," he answered.

"Talk?" I repeated.

Remi nodded. "Have a seat, Kaia."

I sat down, and Remi grabbed one of the chairs, flipped it around, and straddled the seat, resting his forearms over the back of it.

"Okay, so before we get started, I wanted to just talk to you about what you're hoping to accomplish here, how often you want to train, and why you decided to get training in the first place."

Oh. Okay.

I guess that made sense. How could he train me if he didn't even know what I wanted to do?

My head jerked slightly, and I responded, "Right. Well, like I said yesterday, a friend of mine referred me to you. I don't know how much training is typical or recommended, but my goal is to be able to defend myself."

While I didn't exactly lie, I wasn't one-hundred-percent

forthcoming either. I didn't want to tell Remi about Nolan. It wasn't like that would affect the outcome of what I needed to do here anyway.

"Well, we can figure out what kind of schedule will work. You said you work nights. Are you interested in just personal self-defense training, or are you looking for weapons training as well?"

My eyes widened. "Weapons?" I asked.

"Yeah. Do you want to train to use a handgun? We offer CCW classes, which would be required in the state of California to be able to conceal and carry," he explained.

Shaking my head, I assured him, "I'm not looking to shoot anyone. I just want to learn some moves in case I'm ever in a situation."

Remi let out a laugh. "I didn't think you were actively seeking someone to shoot," he started. "If you're not interested in it right now, that's okay. If you change your mind, it's always an option. There's nothing wrong with defensive training."

I nodded my understanding.

"Now, have you ever taken any self-defense classes before?" Remi asked.

"No. This is my first."

"Okay. So, we'll start slow today, and I'll teach you the fundamental techniques that'll help you in nearly every situation. We'll work from there and take this as far as you want to go. I'd be happy to accommodate training for you three mornings a week if that works for you."

"That would be fantastic," I said.

I figured the more training I got, the sooner I would feel less concerned about Nolan's return.

"My recommendation, given that you're new to this,

would be to do Monday, Wednesday, and Friday mornings," he started. "That way, you'll have a day of rest in between to recover."

Recover?

"Are you going to beat me up?" I asked. "What do you mean by recover?"

Remi's face got hard, and his expression turned serious. "I would never beat you up," he assured me, his voice low and stern. "If you don't do it regularly, these training sessions can leave your muscles feeling sore the next day. That's what I mean by recover."

"Oh, that makes sense," I replied sheepishly. "I am okay to do three days a week, but Friday is probably not the best option for me as I work Thursday nights. It might be pushing it to be here by ten in the morning."

Remi thought for a moment and asked, "Would you like to do Monday, Wednesday, and Thursday mornings instead? Or, we could do it a little bit later on Friday. What time would work for you?"

I considered my options. "Monday, Wednesday, and Thursday would probably be the best bet," I told him. Then, something dawned on me, and I said, "But today is Tuesday."

"Yeah, you'd be looking at Tuesday, Wednesday, and Thursday this week if you wanted to get three sessions in," he noted. "We can ease you in so you aren't feeling so sore, or we can just do Tuesday and Thursday this week to give you that time off."

No. I didn't want to waste any time. I'd rather be sore from learning how to do this instead of being sore because Nolan hurt me.

"I want to come three times," I told him.

Something strange washed over Remi. For a moment I thought I imagined it because as soon as I saw it, it was gone.

Then he smiled at me and said in a way that sounded like a promise, "I'll make that happen for you."

I don't know what it was, but there was something about Remi that I just liked a whole lot. He was easygoing, friendly, and accommodating. If he was like this with everyone, I was surprised he had the time to work with me three mornings a week.

"Thank you so much."

"You're welcome," Remi replied. "Now, the next thing I want to do is talk to you a bit like I do to our groups of women who come in for the training seminars as a group. It's important for you to understand all the different types of situations and scenarios that can occur. The goal is not just to make sure you have the physical skills to help you in any situation but also the proper perspective and mental toughness to deal with anything that comes your way."

I stared at him. I don't know what I was expecting would happen today, but this wasn't necessarily it.

"Is everything okay?" he asked.

"Yeah, I just… I guess I just didn't realize that there was more to self-defense training than the actual self-defense," I admitted.

Remi smiled at me again. "The physical aspect of it is an important part of it, but the bigger part of it is your mind. Remaining calm, staying in control, being aware of your surroundings, and not losing your focus are all just as crucial to survival as being able to physically defend yourself."

"That makes sense," I said.

"Good."

For the next fifteen minutes or so, I did my best to pay attention to everything Remi was telling me. He talked a lot about something called situational awareness and how crucial it was to be cognizant of what was happening around me in any instance. By the time he was finished, I would have guessed I had taken in and absorbed about eighty percent of the information he had communicated. The remaining twenty percent might have gotten lost when I found myself focusing on his mouth or his eyes or his impeccable body.

It was all so captivating.

I didn't know what was wrong with me. I was fresh out of a relationship and had no business looking at a man how I was looking at Remi.

What could I say? I wasn't perfect.

When he finished with the lecture portion of the training, Remi suggested, "Okay, so how about we get started with some basic techniques today? We'll start slow and make sure you understand everything."

"That sounds great," I replied.

"Alright. Why don't you drop your bag and meet me on the mat?" he urged.

Meet him on the mat.

I could do that. I could *definitely* do that.

As Remi walked away from me and out onto the mat, I checked out his ass. Then I dropped my bag and quickly hurried after him, silently hoping I'd be able to maintain control over my hormones.

I had to learn how to look out for myself. It was time to get serious.

CHAPTER 6

Kaia

"**R**EMEMBER WHAT I SHOWED YOU. HOW ARE YOU going to get out?"

This wasn't as easy as I thought it was going to be. That's not to say that I thought learning self-defense techniques was going to be easy. But I didn't know the most challenging part of what I was going to have to do would have nothing to do with the actual techniques I was in the process of learning.

It was Thursday, and I was in my second week of training.

No matter the amount of information, defensive tactics, and encouragement Remi had given me for the first five sessions, this sixth one was proving to be the most challenging. In fact, each class I'd come to had tested me more than the one before.

And it was all because of him.

Remi Archer.

Somehow, I'd been managing to push through each class by focusing most of my effort on what he was teaching me, but it hadn't been easy. And I found that when I got home after training, I'd take anywhere from thirty minutes to an hour to run through the things I remembered from the time I'd spent with him that day just to reinforce it. I'd even practice for another hour or so on the days when I didn't have training.

Not only was that part of the commitment I made to myself to not slack on something that was so vitally important to my safety, but it was also a necessity if I didn't want to look like a floundering idiot in front of Remi.

If there was one thing I knew for certain, it was that I didn't want to appear to be a floundering idiot in front of Remi.

The man was intense. But that wasn't all. He was also kind, gentle, reassuring, intelligent, and so very handsome.

Over the course of the last week and a half of sessions, I'd learned a lot. Just as he had said we would, we started off easy with essential striking techniques. And we repeated them more times than I cared to admit. We worked slowly through lots of the basics in those first three sessions last week. That had been the easiest part of the training to this point.

But things changed this week.

For the last three sessions, today included, I felt like I'd been struggling to pay attention and get the full benefit of my private lessons. Because Remi had decided that it was time to start introducing physical attacks. And the problem with that wasn't that I was having some sort of post-traumatic stress reaction and flashbacks to when Nolan had attacked me. In fact, I hadn't thought much about Nolan at all, especially not when I was in training unless I was practicing strikes. In that case, I imagined it was his face I was walloping.

So, it wasn't Nolan, and it wasn't even that the material was challenging.

It was that Remi was the one doing the teaching.

Because again, he was intense, kind, gentle, reassuring, intelligent, and so very handsome.

He had hazel eyes that were close to matching mine, light brown hair that had been naturally highlighted by the sun, and a body that was to die for. It was strong, solid, and powerful.

Beyond that, he'd been in such close proximity to me that I constantly had the masculine scent of him filling my nostrils. And if that wasn't enough to torture a girl, he had put his hands on me. When Remi put his hands on me, it wasn't anything like when Nolan had done it. Even though Remi had been touching me to set up a scenario where I was being attacked, it wasn't violent. Quite frankly, it felt like heaven on earth every time his fingertips landed on my skin, or his arms came around my body.

And I didn't think there was a man or woman on this planet who would have blamed me for struggling just a bit on my concentration when just the close proximity of one person could make me feel something so good, something I'd longed for for so long.

I hadn't felt this good even when things had been good between Nolan and me. That realization had come to me several times this week just before I'd fall asleep. I'd think about how things had been for us from the moment we got together until it all fell apart. And while there were plenty of moments that had been good between us, nothing stood out as extraordinary. Nothing made me feel the way I knew I should have felt when it was the real deal, the way my sister felt when she met the man who was now her husband.

Although it might have been understandable for me to cower away from even the thought of another relationship, I didn't want to. I wanted to be happy, and I wanted someone to share my life with. There was no way I was going to let Nolan take that away from me.

"Come on, Kaia. I know you know what to do," Remi encouraged me.

I did. I knew what to do.

But his solid body was pressing into mine from behind in what had been dubbed the bear hug attack, his arms were wrapped around me, and all I wanted to do was stay right there where I felt safe. And desire. And warmth.

I knew I couldn't stay there, though.

So, just like he'd demonstrated to me when he had me pretend to be the attacker yesterday, I created the space for myself by leveraging my weight. I leaned forward, got as low as I could, made that space between us, and turned into him using one of my elbows. It connected with his face, his hold on me loosened, and I was able to turn enough to bring a hand to his back, one to his neck, and a knee to the groin. Of course, I never actually connected my knee to his groin, but I understood what I needed to do.

"That was the best one yet," Remi praised me. "You had me worried there for a second. I thought you'd forgotten what to do."

No, I just wanted you to keep holding me, I thought.

"I was trying to make you think you had won," I teased.

Remi laughed and said, "Well, I can tell you that if you fully executed all those moves and did them with force behind them, I have no doubt you would have been successful. Your attacker's ego would have gotten the best of him if he'd gotten you in that hold and thought he won."

"Do you really think so?" I asked, genuinely curious about his confidence in my ability.

"Absolutely."

I felt a bit of relief at his statement, but something still bothered me. Remi must have noticed my mind working because he asked, "Is something wrong?"

Shaking my head, I confessed, "I don't know. I just... well, I really wonder if I'd be effective in a real-life situation. My guess is that you aren't attacking me the way someone who was trying to hurt me would, so I guess it's just making me doubt whether I could actually take a guy down and best him."

"You won't," he deadpanned.

My eyes widened in shock. Well, that stung.

"Kaia, listen to me," he urged. There was something in his voice that told me he was desperate for me to listen and understand what he was about to say. When he had my full attention, he explained, "The goal of what you're trying to do here isn't besting the guy and doing as much damage to him as you can possibly manage. The goal is for you to do what's necessary to disengage from your attacker and get away. When it comes to physical size and strength, a male attacker will likely have the advantage in most cases. But that doesn't mean you can't do what's necessary to protect yourself. You just need to be smart. Disengage from him by whatever means necessary using any of the techniques I've already shown you, or what you still have yet to learn, and get away. That's your goal. Escape the attacker and get yourself somewhere safe."

For a brief moment, the night Nolan attacked me in the

kitchen when I came home from work popped into my head. I tried to get away. All I wanted to do was get out of there. Perhaps I waited too long by engaging in conversation with him, but once he started attacking, I focused only on getting away and surviving. Now that I'd had these classes, I realized that my mindset throughout most of the attack had been what it should have been. I just didn't have the knowledge of how to physically protect myself in a situation like that.

And now I did.

Or, at least, I was well on my way to learning it all.

"I understand," I promised him.

"Are you sure?" he pressed.

Nodding, I confirmed, "Yes, Remi, I do."

With my assurance in hand, he shared, "I get what you're saying. We'll work on full-blown defensive techniques where you can follow through after you get a bit more practice in. And yes, I'm not attacking you the way an attacker would, so you are correct. Right now, I want you to learn what you need to know without being overwhelmed by the force of a real attack."

I considered telling him that I'd already felt myself on the brink of death during an attack. I wondered if the feeling of having my breath stolen or the sharp edge of a knife pressed against my throat gave me the full effect of what a real attack was like. Did it get worse? Could it? I thought I was going to die in those moments, so I wasn't sure how much worse I could feel during another attack.

I was so lost in my thoughts about those moments I feared for my life that I didn't realize the change that had come over me.

Remi didn't miss it.

And the next thing I knew, I felt his hand give my shoulder a gentle squeeze as he softly called, "Kaia?"

I lifted my gaze to his.

Something was swirling in his eyes as he assured me, "No matter how intense our training gets, I would never allow it to get to a point where you end up hurt. I want you to know that."

"I do," I rasped, feeling something stirring inside of me.

He nodded slowly and insisted, "We'll work up to that point. It's not happening today or even next week. Trust me when I tell you that I'm not going to put you in that position until I know you're ready for it."

I bit my lip and belatedly noticed Remi's eyes drop to it.

I couldn't focus on that, though. This man had no idea what his words meant to me. To know that he'd seen my reaction to his earlier statement and assumed I was worried I'd end up hurt, and his only concern was reassuring me that he'd never allow that to happen was everything.

"Thank you," I finally whispered. I swallowed hard, and with a bit more conviction in my tone, I added, "I'm looking forward to learning more so we can get to that point."

"We will," he replied, giving my shoulder another squeeze. Following a brief pause, he said, "Good work today, Kaia. I'm really impressed by how quickly you're learning and your determination to keep going. Next week should be really exciting."

"Thanks, Remi. I can't wait," I told him. "For now, I better head out and get some rest in before I have to go to work tonight. But I'll see you on Monday morning."

"Sounds great," he returned with a smile.

After I rounded up my things, I moved to the door of the

room we'd been training in and stopped. With my hand on the doorknob, I turned back to look at Remi and said, "Have a good weekend."

"You, too. Goodbye, Kaia."

"Bye."

With that, I opened the door and walked out feeling the best I had in a really long time. And I knew I had Remi to thank for that.

"I heard what happened with you and Nolan, and I'm so sorry. Bianca told me the other night. I've wanted to talk to you and make sure you're okay, but it's been so crazy here. We're all devastated for you."

That came from Skylar. It was Saturday night and the first night I'd really had a chance to talk to her for more than a few seconds, like when she was bringing me a drink to the booth.

I'd arrived at work just a few minutes ago and was a bit early. So, when I was walking by the bar and saw her there, I decided to stop and catch up. I should have prepared myself for this.

Even though I'd already told Bianca that I was okay and the breakup was for the best, Skylar wouldn't care. She was a good friend, and she would be worried. So, I should have expected she'd want to talk to me about it on her own.

"I'm okay," I assured her. "Really. It was a good thing, and I'm actually really happy right now."

"Are you sure?" she pressed. "I thought you two were cute together."

"I'm sure," I returned. "This was a final thing between us, too. There's no chance we'll work it out and get back together at some point down the road. We're officially over. But I promise I'm okay with it and not drowning my sorrows in vats of popcorn and chocolate."

Skylar let out a laugh. "Well, that's good news then. All that matters to me is that you're happy," she said. "I've got to get back to it now, but we'll talk later. And we need to plan a girls' night."

"Absolutely," I agreed. "I'm flexible, so you two let me know what works for you."

"Sounds good. Have a killer night tonight, Kaia."

"Thank you."

With that, I continued my trek across the room at Club Infinity and saw Juan there. Ever since I told him I'd started getting self-defense lessons from Remi at Archer Tactical, I noticed Juan was a bit more relaxed. Of course, relaxed when it came to Juan only meant so much considering the man was generally on alert. He still saw me home safely every night I worked, even though I'd insisted he was going overboard. I hadn't heard anything from Nolan. Part of me had hoped that perhaps he'd come to the conclusion I wasn't worth the effort, and he decided to move on. The other part of me wasn't convinced I was that lucky. Nevertheless, it didn't stop me from hoping that was the case.

As I approached the booth with a bit of a hop in my step, I thought I could do something to ease Juan's mind just a bit more. I still had a few minutes left before I needed to get started, so I took my chance.

"Can you do me a favor?" I asked as I walked up to him.

"Sure, what do you need?" he replied.

I held one finger up and said, "Give me one minute."

I dashed up the steps, dropped my things in the booth,

and walked back out. I came back down the stairs, looked up at Juan, and grinned. Then, I claimed, "I bet I can surprise you tonight."

His brows pulled together. "What?"

"A surprise. I bet I can surprise you," I repeated.

"What are the terms?" he asked.

"If I win, you don't need to escort me home tonight," I told him.

"Banks—"

I held my hand up in front of me and cut him off. "Juan, you've got to trust me."

I'm not sure if he said it to appease me or if he was actually going to follow through and grant my request when I won the bet, but he replied, "Alright, what is it?"

"Attack me."

"What?" he returned, his voice filled with shock.

Suffice it to say, I felt like I'd already won, considering I nearly knocked him off his feet with my demand. Instead of gloating over that, I laughed and explained, "Not seriously. I just want to show you something. Bear hug attack from behind."

Then, I turned myself around so my back was to him.

I stood there for a few moments waiting for Juan to make his move. I was sure he was thinking about whether to follow through. Or maybe he was just getting reinforcement that I was a crazy woman. Either way, I knew he wouldn't let me down, so I waited patiently.

Sure enough, I eventually felt Juan's arms come around me. And with what felt like lightning-quick reflexes, I escaped the hold.

When I was standing before him with a proud smile on my face, he didn't hesitate to offer some praise.

"Color me impressed, Banks. That was incredible."

"Thank you."

"But I'm still escorting you home," he shared.

I gasped. "What? Did you just see what I did?"

"Yep. And it was good. I'm happy to see how hard you're working and even happier to see you smiling and joking again. But I'm still not taking any chances."

My shoulders fell, and I sighed.

"Fine," I grumbled as I made my way back up to the booth.

As the night wore on, I glanced out at Juan and offered puppy dog eyes. I wasn't against doing anything to relieve him of this duty he felt obligated to uphold. I could tell by the look in his eyes that he wasn't going to budge.

So, I accepted my fate and got lost in my work. It wasn't hard considering how good I'd been feeling over the last week.

And just when I thought things couldn't get any better, I looked out into the crowd as I often did and locked eyes with him.

Remi was standing there among a crowd of people, and yet, it was like he was the only one in the room. He was staring at me and there was a smile on his face that I'd never seen before. Yes, he'd smiled at me throughout our training sessions but never like he was now.

I couldn't help myself.

I smiled back and waved him over.

CHAPTER 7

Remi

I DIDN'T WANT TO DO THIS.

But if I had any hope of not being called out by my brothers, I had no choice. We were going out tonight, and I was currently on my way to meet Vaughn and Deacon.

It wasn't like it would all be bad. It was just that I didn't have any desire to follow through on what I knew they had planned tonight.

And the thing about all of it was that they knew where my head was at, even if I hadn't officially admitted it to them. In fact, they had pushed me to go out mostly because they knew I was lost entirely in Kaia and our training sessions.

They had no problem giving me a hard time about it either.

Following the session I had with her on Thursday morning, they started. At first, I thought they were just being curious and supportive, but I quickly learned that wasn't entirely the case.

"How is Kaia doing?" Deacon asked when I approached them in the break room.

There was a bit of downtime since Kaia and I had spent a few extra minutes working together, and it was essentially lunchtime by the time we finished.

"Really good," I told them. "She's picked everything up very quickly, and she's determined to perfect everything."

"That's cool," Vaughn said. "She seems like she's focused. You guys were in there a little longer today."

Nodding, I sat down at the table and confirmed, "Yeah, Kaia knows she won't be back until Monday, so we wanted a few more minutes to practice."

"And you didn't mind accommodating her request," Deacon goaded me.

"Nope."

"Have you asked her out on a date yet?" he pressed.

I shook my head.

"What are you waiting for?" Vaugh wondered.

"I'm keeping it professional for right now," I started. "She wants to learn, not be harassed by the guy that's supposed to be teaching her."

"She hasn't indicated that she's interested?" Deacon asked curiously.

Letting out a laugh, I said, "I know this is hard to believe, but not every woman that walks through the door is interested in something more than just the professional services we offer."

My brother narrowed his eyes on me. "Are you saying you only want to offer her professional services?"

"I didn't say that."

"So, what are you waiting for?"

I shrugged because I didn't exactly have an answer for

that. I didn't know what I was waiting for. Sure, part of me was telling them that I was trying to keep it professional. But I knew that wasn't the full truth.

I'd never met anyone like Kaia, and the more that I was around her, the more I wanted to know about her.

But things hadn't gotten that far between us. For the most part, our training sessions had kept us busy discussing and implementing self-defense techniques. When Kaia had questions, I answered them. Beyond that, I didn't really know her.

I did know that I liked her.

A lot.

And for the time being, I enjoyed what I had with her, even though I could have easily considered it torture. Being in such close proximity to her every morning we trained was taking its toll, and my resolve to keep it professional was undoubtedly waning.

All I wanted to do every time I put her in a hold was spin her around so her chest was pressed against mine, tighten my arms around her, and kiss her senseless. I never wanted to let her go. That was the part of me that hated that I was teaching her how to escape a hold.

Of course, I wanted her to know what to do if she was ever in a bad situation, but if she was ever with me, she'd never have to worry about that.

And since I didn't have an answer for my brother's question, Deacon insisted, "Then I guess you're still going out with us this weekend."

"I don't know. I'm really not feeling it," I responded.

That's when Vaughn cut in and suggested, "But maybe it'll be just what you need."

"How so?" I asked.

"If you go out with us and don't find what you're looking for, maybe that will be the kick in the pants you need to do something about Kaia," he reasoned.

He did have a point.

Given that I had been holding myself back from getting to know her better when she seemed to be all I could think about lately, I decided to give in and agreed to go.

So, now I was here, on my way to meet up with Vaughn and Deacon. I didn't know for sure who had come up with the idea, but they told me yesterday at work that we'd be meeting up at Club Infinity in Poppy Valley.

I was born and raised in Ventura, the most prominent California city closest to Poppy Valley. Archer Tactical had always been in Poppy Valley, and my brothers and I all lived here now.

Years ago, I'd gone out and come to the club, but I hadn't been back since. And if I got my way, I had a feeling I wouldn't be spending much time here in the future. If I was lucky, I'd be spending my free time with Kaia.

The thought of her made me smile. I hated that I had to wait until Monday to see her again. Monday, Wednesday, and Thursday mornings were the highlights of my week. I looked forward to spending that time with her, even if it wasn't all the way I had wanted it.

I didn't think anyone could blame me for wanting more time with her. I was intrigued by so much about her and had yet to find anything I didn't like about her. She has an incredibly fiery spirit, a determined mindset, a fantastic body, and she smells great. As I told my brothers, she's also a fast learner who isn't afraid to try anything I show her.

From where I was standing, Kaia was perfect for me.

And, on the surface, she was everything I'd been looking for.

How I knew that but I didn't even know what she did for a living was beyond me. I didn't care, though. I'd spend the time teaching her what she needed to know, and once I was confident that she had all the tools she needed, I'd make my move. That's when I'd get to know her.

No sooner had I parked in the club's lot when I spotted Vaughn and Deacon. They were both already on their way to the front door. I got out, let out a whistle, and saw them stop. Turning around, they found me, and I jerked my chin up at them.

A few minutes later, the three of us were inside and had grabbed ourselves a couple of drinks. We managed to snag one of the exclusive booths, which put us in an excellent position to do a lot of observing. Truth be told, it didn't really matter much to me because I didn't expect I'd be doing much watching anyway.

A couple hours later, I found I was right.

This was not the place for me. Both of my brothers had talked to some women throughout the evening, but I wasn't interested in finding anyone else.

Of course, that also meant that Vaughn was also right.

Coming here was the kick in the pants I needed to do something about Kaia. As I sat there waiting for the night to be over, though, I found myself wishing I'd talked to her like I had wanted to on Thursday. Now I was subjected to hours of this. If nothing else, at least the two drinks had been good, and the music was killer.

Just as I had decided to call it quits for the night, Vaughn returned from the bathroom and asked, "Hey, Remi, did you know?"

"Know what?" I returned.

He lifted his hand and pointed off to the side. Our booth had been located around the middle of the vast space, and Vaughn's finger was indicating the wall all the way off to my left.

My eyes followed the direction he was pointing, and I instantly froze.

There, dancing in the DJ booth, was Kaia.

I was captivated by her. Was there anything she couldn't do?

All night long, I'd thought about how decent the music had been, and it never dawned on me to look up at the booth. She'd been here the entire time.

Without taking my eyes off of her, I started to move out from behind the table in our booth. As I did that, I answered Vaughn, "I had no idea."

"Where are you going?" Deacon asked as he rejoined us.

"Don't wait around for me," I told him. "I found the girl I'm taking home tonight."

"Who?" he wondered.

I jerked my chin in the direction of Kaia and said, "Her."

Then, without waiting for his response, I started moving through the crowd of people to get a better view of her.

God, she was incredible, and I was mesmerized.

For the next few minutes, I simply stood there and watched her, loving everything I was seeing. She was so carefree and happy and completely in her element.

I don't know how long I had been watching her when she looked in my direction and locked gazes with me. Unsure of how she'd react, I braced myself. Much to my surprise, her face lit up, and she waved me over toward her.

Yep.

I was taking this girl home tonight.

As I made my way across the room, I realized the entrance to her booth had to be on the opposite side of where I'd been sitting all night. I started moving in that direction, keeping my body on the perimeter of the crowd. Then, I spotted a familiar face.

Juan.

Juan had done his security training at Archer Tactical. I had to admit it felt good to know that he was the guy standing guard just outside the booth that held the woman who'd sparked an interest in me like no woman had before her.

He saw me approaching, and his mouth twitched as he jerked his chin up at me. When I came to a stop in front of him, he held out his hand and said, "Remi, my man, it's been a while," he greeted me.

My hand met his as I replied, "It's good to see you, Juan. How's it going?"

Before he could respond, the door to the DJ booth opened, and Kaia stuck her head out. "Come on up," she urged.

As much as I didn't want to, I looked away from her and returned my attention to Juan. "We'll talk later," I said.

He chuckled. "No problem."

With that, I climbed a couple of stairs and joined Kaia in her booth.

The second the door closed, she put her arms around me and gave me a hug. It stunned me briefly, and I found I couldn't focus until she took a step back and said, "I didn't think I was going to see you until Monday. What are you doing here? Did you find out that this is where I work?"

Shaking my head, I answered, "No, my brothers wanted to come out tonight. I came against my will."

She let out a laugh. "I still have to meet them," she declared. "I'm so embarrassed I walked in and ignored them that first day."

I grinned at her and insisted, "Trust me, they aren't mad at you."

Kaia held up one finger and said, "Give me just a second."

Giving her a simple nod, I replied, "Sure."

With that, she turned around and got back to doing her thing. I took that opportunity to stand back and admire the view.

Fuck.

Gorgeous didn't even cut it.

Kaia was wearing a black dress that seemed to be made of satin and showed off her gorgeous, toned legs. It wasn't super tight to her body, though. It fit her loose, like a smaller version of an oversized sleep shirt. But where a sleep shirt would do nothing for her figure, this dress was a mix of sexy and edgy.

Every time Kaia had come in for self-defense training, she'd been wearing leggings, so I knew she had a beautiful body. But now that I was seeing her bare skin, I felt a little off-balance. If that wasn't already more than I could handle, I now had to watch her move that body as she got lost in the music and her work.

This woman was everything.

Everything.

After some time passed, she turned back to me and asked, "So, what do you think? Is this what you expected?"

"You mean, did I think you were a DJ?" I returned.

"Yeah."

"Nope. Not at all," I replied. "I'm thoroughly impressed, Kaia. This is awesome."

"Thank you. Though, I guess I'm a little surprised," she returned.

"Surprised?"

Nodding, she explained, "I figure that somebody like you has the resources and capability to find out something as simple as where I work."

Letting out a laugh, I reasoned, "If that's what I had been trying to do, I would have just asked you."

She pursed her lips and furrowed her brows. I'd never seen anything more adorable.

Not wanting her to have the wrong impression, I shared, "For what it's worth, I didn't ask because I was trying to remain professional."

Kaia shot an assessing look my way as she cocked an eyebrow. She turned around and got back to her work. I wondered if that was my cue to leave the booth, but just as I was about to make that move, she looked back over her shoulder at me and smiled.

Nope.

No way was I leaving.

I'd let her do her thing and be completely happy watching her bare legs and sexy body move around.

When the night finally ended, I was still content being right where I was, watching Kaia in her element. For the first time since they dragged me here, I was grateful to my brothers. I had needed this more than I could have ever imagined.

After Kaia had packed up all her things, she opened the

door, and we descended the stairs. Though I guess I shouldn't have been, I was surprised to see Juan was still there.

"So, you two already know each other," Kaia declared.

I wondered how she knew that, but then it dawned on me that she'd said a friend of hers had recommended her to me. Knowing Juan like I did, I found that strange. Unless Kaia specifically said she wanted self-defense lessons, Juan did not strike me as the kind of guy who went around giving out referrals to Archer Tactical for no reason. Then again, Kaia had surprised me, so I realized she might have decided to take up training.

"Yes, we do," Juan confirmed. Turning his attention to me, he said, "I cannot tell you how happy I am to know that you're working here with Banks, Remi. I knew she needed the best of the best to help her, so I'm glad she finally listened to me and came to you. At least now, she'll be ready."

He took a moment to pause and returned his gaze to Kaia. "So, is he escorting you home, or am I?"

"Um—"

That was all Kaia got out before I asked Juan, "What do you mean?"

That made no sense. Why would Juan escort her home?

"Guys—" Kaia started but was cut off by Juan.

Shaking his head with a look of disgust on his face, he answered, "I can't do it, man. She changed the locks, but I don't trust that guy. I never did. And I won't take that chance and assume that he won't be there waiting for her again when she gets home."

My gut clenched. I didn't know what was going on, but I'd heard enough to know I wasn't going to like the rest of the story. My eyes shot to Kaia's, and I could see fear written all over her face.

"Shit," Juan hissed. "You didn't tell him, did you, Banks?"

"No," she whispered her reply.

That's when I knew. Kaia hadn't just come to Archer Tactical because she wanted to be prepared if she was ever attacked.

She came because it had already happened.

CHAPTER 8

Kaia

"TELL ME WHAT?"

Damn it. Why did I make such a stupid decision?

I had acted entirely on impulse and good vibes. When I looked out into the crowd and saw Remi looking—no, *gazing*—at me like he was, I couldn't help myself. I had to wave him up here. I got caught up in everything I'd been feeling and just had to invite him up into the booth with me.

The truth was, the whole thing had thrown me for a loop as well. I mean, the fact that I couldn't have just smiled and waved and continued to do my thing struck me as odd. Why couldn't I have just let him enjoy his night out with his brothers?

I knew why.

It was because I hadn't expected to see him until Monday morning, and I simply didn't think before I acted. Today had already been such a good day, and there was too much excitement pulsing through me. Once I saw him, it took everything up another notch for me.

I liked the fact that he was going to know something more about me other than just the fact that I was a girl who was being taught how to defend herself. I liked it so much, I even hugged the man the moment he was inside the booth.

What had come over me?

Of course, in all of that, I ignored everything he'd taught me about awareness. God, what would he think now that he knew I hadn't fully considered the situation? I was probably the worst student that ever came through Archer Tactical.

I never intended for Remi to learn about Nolan. At least, not now. And if I was completely honest, maybe not ever.

Obviously, if something happened and I needed his advice or something, I might have told him, but it was the last thing I wanted to do. Besides, Nolan hadn't attempted to contact me since the night he attacked me. It had been more than two weeks. I was still holding out hope that perhaps he'd decided to move on with his life. Beyond that, aside from the fact that Nolan's attack was the whole reason I ended up at Archer Tactical for self-defense training, I hadn't really thought about him much. In the rare moments that I did, it wasn't ever when I was talking to Remi. Yes, I'd imagined it was Nolan I was striking when Remi was teaching me, but that was it.

Now, I had no choice but to tell Remi the horrible, ugly truth.

Looking at his handsome face as he shifted his attention between Juan and me, I could see it. Even without any explanation, he'd already figured it out. Maybe he didn't know all the specifics, but he knew. And from what I could see, he didn't like one thing about it.

"Tell me what?" Remi repeated.

I watched as Juan opened his mouth to speak, but I cut him off.

"Juan?" I called.

His eyes came to mine. In them, I saw a mix of confusion and anguish. He was confused because he probably didn't understand why I never shared the full truth with Remi. There was no doubt the sorrow was all because he had shared something personal about me not realizing I hadn't already revealed it.

I didn't blame him, and I wasn't mad at him. I knew he only wanted the best for me and was too excited when he saw Remi not to say something to him about it. So, I tried to offer him a reassuring look before I asked, "Can you give us a minute, please?"

He dipped his chin. "Sure."

With that, I moved back up the stairs and into the booth. As I set my things down, Remi came in and closed the door. When I turned around, I saw him watching me with an edge of trepidation in his expression.

As much as he verbally demanded an answer to his question, he really didn't want to know. But being the kind of guy he was, not knowing wasn't an option for him. That was why his voice sounded so firm and unwavering when he asked what I hadn't told him. But I could see it in his eyes. They were pleading with me to tell him anything other than what he already assumed was the truth.

I couldn't.

So, I didn't.

Instead, I took a deep breath and explained, "I came to

Archer Tactical to get self-defense training because I had already been attacked."

Remi's body, which had already held so much tension, grew even more rigid. Regardless of whatever thoughts or questions he might have had, he didn't speak.

I continued, "It happened twice. They were both bad, but the second one was much scarier. Wednesday night, two weeks ago, I'd gotten into an argument with my ex-boyfriend. Technically, we hadn't officially ended things at that point. It was the first time he'd ever been violent with me. And we'd been together for nearly a year. I'd returned a few days prior from a trip to visit my sister and her new baby. I'd been gone for two weeks, a trip I extended not long after I got there. That Wednesday night after I returned, he got upset because I was still gushing over my new niece and apparently, not giving him the attention he thought he deserved. I ended up with a cut lip and a bruised cheek that night. And I foolishly assumed he understood when he left that night that we were over."

Remi closed his eyes and let out a sigh. Either this was affecting him more than I thought it would and he needed a moment to come to terms with all of it, or he was attempting to prepare himself for what I still needed to share.

I thought it was best to be sure he wanted me to continue, so I asked, "Do you… are you sure you want me to share the rest?"

There wasn't an ounce of hesitation in his tone when he answered, "I want to know everything."

I nodded my understanding and was about to start again when he suggested, "I think we should get out of here first, though. It sounds to me as though Juan's been seeing you home safely. Would you mind if I took over the position tonight?"

"I tried showing him tonight when I got here how good I was at getting out of a bear hug attack just to get him to stop feeling obligated to make sure I made it home safe," I murmured.

"Did he agree?" Remi asked.

I shook my head. "No. And since I think Juan needs the relief, the job is yours tonight if you want it."

"Get your things," he urged gently.

I didn't move. I was too captivated by the tenderness in his voice. As solid and tough as Remi's exterior was, I never expected he could sound so gentle. At that moment, it was precisely what I needed. If I was going to tell him about the rest of what happened, all of it, I needed the reassurance that he wasn't going to fly off the handle.

He had no idea what he'd just given me. I closed my eyes and fought to keep the tears at bay.

"Kaia?" he called.

The care and concern in his voice was almost too much to take. Somehow, I managed to keep it together, though. I opened my eyes and locked them on his. Remi took two steps toward me, closing the distance between us. His hand reached for mine at my side. Holding it there, he stroked his thumb softly across my knuckles for a few seconds. Then he squeezed lightly and repeated, "Get your things so we can get you home."

"Okay," I rasped.

This time, I moved.

A moment later, we were descending the stairs from the booth again. Juan was waiting at the bottom.

I felt so bad for him when I noted the look on his face.

It killed him to know he'd shared something that wasn't his to share. I put a hand to his arm and said, "It's okay, Juan. I promise. Thank you for giving me the push I needed."

"Banks, you know I'd never—"

"I know," I assured him, cutting him off. "I promise it's okay. Remi is going to follow me home tonight."

Juan's eyes went to Remi's.

A look of mutual respect passed between the men, and Remi held his hand out to Juan. They shook hands as Remi said, "I knew I always liked you, Juan. You're a good man."

Juan returned, "I could say the same about you." He jerked his head toward me and demanded, "Take care of her."

"You have my word."

With that, Remi put his hand to the small of my back and ushered me away. I was acutely aware of his touch as we walked toward the exit and out of the building.

As we walked through the parking lot, Remi offered, "If you aren't up for driving, I'd be happy to take you home tonight. I can come back tomorrow morning and pick you up so you can get your car."

"No, that's okay," I replied. "I appreciate the offer, but that'll just be a bigger hassle for you. I can drive home. It's not that far anyway."

"Whatever you want," he said. "But just so you know, it would not be a hassle or an inconvenience to me at all. Okay?"

I looked up at him as we came to a stop beside my car and offered a small smile. Remi reached out and opened my door for me. As soon as I folded myself in behind the wheel, he said, "I'm around the front."

"If you want to get in, I can drive you there," I told him. "That way, you can just follow right behind me."

At that, Remi closed my door and rounded the car. Then he got in on the opposite side. I took him around the front to his car and gave him a moment to get in and back out of the spot before I pulled away and drove to my apartment.

My mind was racing throughout the entire drive home. I didn't know how this was going to go with Remi. I'd had a million thoughts about different scenarios that included him, particularly over the last week, but none of them involved telling him about this.

He'd already shown me that he could be sweet and attentive during a difficult or tense situation. I just hoped there wasn't a limit to how much he could actually handle before that good-natured attitude shifted into something else. He didn't seem like the type that would ever allow that to happen, especially considering his line of work. But I'd have been lying if I didn't admit that I never thought Nolan had it in him either.

My thoughts kept me so occupied that I was opening the door to my apartment and welcoming Remi inside before I knew it. Once he closed and locked the door, I asked, "Did you want something to drink?"

He shook his head.

"Okay, well, have a seat," I urged, extending my hand to the sofa.

Remi moved toward it and sat down. I planted myself on the opposite side and removed my shoes. Then I tucked my feet underneath my booty and turned toward him. Even though his gaze didn't linger creepily, I couldn't miss the fact that Remi had been looking at my legs. I had to admit I liked it.

In my dream world, the one I'd been living in all week,

Remi looking at my legs like he had been would have led to something much more exciting and fulfilling. Unfortunately, I wasn't living in a dream world. This was reality, and I needed to face it.

"Kaia?" Remi called, pulling me out of my thoughts.

"Yeah?"

"Tell me what happened on Thursday," he urged.

I took in a deep breath and let out a sigh. Then I shared, "I came home from work around this time on that Thursday. I never expected him to be here. I know now how stupid that was, but I just didn't think he would have returned. He was never the kind of guy to just show up here anyway. We always planned it."

I paused a moment before I went on, "Anyway, I had gone into the kitchen to grab a glass of water when he walked in from the bedroom and acted like everything was as it had always been. I immediately told him to leave, but he wouldn't go. Things started to get heated between us, and every time he advanced, I retreated. I kept moving back until I had nowhere else to go because the stove was behind me. So, I made a split-second decision and tried to climb over the counter to get away. I never made it."

Up to this point, I'd been doing okay. This was really the first time I'd relived what happened that night. Even though Juan knew what had happened, he didn't know the full extent of the story because I never shared it.

Now, I was going to share it, and I could already feel myself growing anxious.

"We scuffled for a bit," I began again. "He pulled my hair, I pushed him away, he pinned me against the fridge, stuff like that. Since I wasn't strong enough to move him away from me, I started screaming, hoping I'd wake one of the neighbors. That's when he backhanded me across the face and told me to shut up. He'd loosened his hold enough that I was able to start moving away, but he caught me again. And before I knew it, I was on my back on the floor. He got on top of me and…" I trailed off.

I swallowed hard and closed my eyes, remembering the fear that I felt as he started to squeeze the life out of me.

Suddenly, I heard movement, and my eyes shot open. Remi had shifted himself closer to me on the couch. He took my hand in his and gave it a squeeze. I appreciated the gesture more than I could have ever communicated. All I wanted was to continue to feel that, to feel the tenderness and sweet affection from Remi. His touch brought me a comfort I never could have imagined.

"Kaia?"

I opened my eyes and saw the worry in his. "Yeah?"

"Did he take advantage of you?" he asked, his voice deeper and huskier than usual.

My God, I hadn't realized how much this was affecting him. As hard as it was to hear him so affected by what I was sharing and what he thought had happened, it was also the most beautiful thing I'd ever experienced. He barely knew me, and this was having such a profound effect on him.

"No," I answered.

Some of the tension left Remi's body. He was relieved to know I hadn't been raped, but it was clear he still anticipated what was coming.

"He nearly killed me, though," I blurted.

I hadn't meant to say it like that, but it just flew out of my mouth. And in an instant, the rigidity was present in Remi's body again.

Feeling my emotions getting the best of me, my eyes welled with tears as I rasped, "I continued to kick and scream. He wanted me to be quiet. Since I wouldn't listen to him, he started to choke me. I was gasping for breath and was convinced I was going to pass out just as my neighbor knocked on my door."

"Thank fuck," he muttered.

"He didn't stop," I shared.

"What?"

Shaking my head, I recalled what happened. "He loosened his hold on my throat, which allowed me to take in some air through my nose, but he kept his hand over my mouth. Clara, my neighbor, shouted through the door and asked if I was okay. Nolan told her that we were moving furniture."

Remi's brows shot up. "She believed that?"

"No, which is why she continued to call my name and ask if I was okay," I answered. "It wasn't until she said she thought it would be best to call the police just to be sure that he removed his hand from my mouth."

"Did you tell her you needed help?"

"No," I whispered.

"Why not?" he pressed.

"Because he might have removed his hand from my mouth so I could speak, but he replaced it with a knife at my throat."

There was a moment of silence as he took that in. I slowly closed my eyes, and tears fell down my cheeks.

"I thought I was going to die," I rasped. "I didn't think I'd ever see my sister, my brother-in-law, or my niece ever again. I thought my sister was going to have to come and identify my body. I've never been so scared before in all my life."

Just like that, the minute I got it out, I burst into tears. I hated that I was crying. I hated that Remi was seeing me like this, but I couldn't hold it in any longer.

I barely had the opportunity to bury my face in my hands when Remi tugged me forward into his arms. He held me tight, one of his hands stroking up and down my back.

"Get it out, Kaia," he encouraged me.

The tenderness in his touch and the gentle tone of his voice only served to make me cry harder.

Remi shifted us on the couch with incredible ease, so our bodies were pressed together, my front against his. He kept his arms wrapped firmly around me while I kept my face buried in his chest. And for a long time, he didn't say anything. He just let me do what I needed to do to get it out.

Once I did, which took a while, I confessed, "This makes me feel safe."

"What does?"

"Being in your arms."

Remi responded by pulling me a little closer and holding me a little tighter. Feeling safe and warm, I snuggled closer.

And before I could stop it from happening, my eyes drifted shut, and I fell asleep.

What I didn't know was that it took Remi a lot longer to find sleep.

CHAPTER 9

Remi

MY RIGHT SHOULDER WAS KILLING ME.

For the last hour, I'd been dealing with massive pain as a result of the position I was in, but I didn't dare move.

Nope.

If I had to endure another three hours of pain, I would do it. Mainly because being in my arms made her feel safe.

Sometime in the early morning hours, Kaia had hooked her leg over me, and I wasn't going to do anything to disrupt that. Not a damn thing. I was just going to have to deal with the pain in my shoulder.

The tradeoff wasn't bad, and that was putting it mildly. The truth was, I found myself forgetting about any pain I felt when I focused on the fact that Kaia's body was pressed up against mine, and she wasn't trying to use any of the moves I taught her to get away.

Nope.

Kaia was completely relaxed.

And I loved everything about how that felt.

So, while I enjoyed having her plastered to me like she was—me on my right side, her on her left, and our bodies running the length of one another, other than her leg that was hooked over my hip—I found something else to distract me from the ache I felt in my shoulder. That wasn't exactly difficult to do, considering everything that had happened last night. As much as I would have liked to simply focus on her admission just before she fell asleep about how it made her feel safe to be in my arms, that wasn't what filled my thoughts. Instead, the conversation I had with Kaia before that kept replaying in my mind.

I couldn't get over what she'd been through. In fact, I surprised myself when I somehow managed to keep it together while she shared her story about what happened to her at the hands of her ex-boyfriend. It sickened me to think that she'd been hurt, that the coward had raised his hands to her at all, but it was worse when I thought about her being choked and having a knife held to her throat.

If I ever saw the guy, I wasn't sure I'd be able to hold myself back. Yes, I knew my training would kick in and stop me from making a stupid decision, but I knew it wouldn't prevent me from having the overwhelming urge to rip the guy to shreds for hurting and scaring Kaia.

Now that I knew the truth, I was going to have to figure out how to proceed with her. I had a million questions for her last night, but after the way she broke down in my arms, I didn't want to put her through anything else immediately. At that point, I knew I wasn't going anywhere and would spend the night with her.

And as long as I was with her, nobody else was going to get to her.

She was so strong, and I hated to think that she'd been carrying this around all this time on her own. Obviously, I knew that Juan knew what had happened to her, and I was grateful to him for making sure she did something to protect herself. But I still wished she would have told me sooner.

I was so lost in my thoughts about Kaia and what she'd gone through that I hadn't been paying attention. It wasn't until she started humming in her sleep that I realized my fingertips were gently stroking along the bare skin of her arm.

Yes, now that I was awake, I kept my hands in the appropriate places. When I first woke up, I found my left hand was placed possessively on her ass cheek. As much as I wanted to keep it there, that wasn't the kind of guy I was.

There was no doubt I wanted my hands on her like that, but I wasn't going to do it while she was asleep. I wanted Kaia awake, fully aware, and practically begging for me to touch her. Until that time, I was going to be a gentleman.

So, I had moved my hand to her arm. And apparently, while I thought about everything this beautiful woman had been through over the last two weeks, I had absentmindedly started stroking the skin on her arm.

Based on the noises she was making—sweet humming— she was enjoying my touch.

Several moments later, Kaia started to stir, and as she began to stretch, she pressed her core forward. I couldn't help myself, and I groaned.

I might have had every intention of being a gentleman, but that didn't mean I wasn't fighting a losing battle with trying to keep my cock from reacting to her. The woman was exquisite.

Suddenly, Kaia's entire body grew tense, and her movements stopped. I chanced a glance down toward her face, which was mere inches from my chest, and watched as her eyes shot open. It took her all of a few seconds to assess the situation and realize where she was and who she was with.

Then, like a flash, her head shot back, and her gaze met mine. Her eyes widened as she pressed her palm into my chest and removed her leg that had been thrown over my hip.

As Kaia sat up, she lamented, "Oh my God. I'm so sorry." Her hand came up to cover her mouth while she sat motionless on the edge of the couch. I used the opportunity to lift myself up and allow the blood to flow back into my right arm.

Once I was sitting up beside her, I leaned in and whispered, "It's okay. How are you feeling this morning?"

"Horrified," she mumbled behind her hand.

I brought my hand to her wrist and gently removed it from in front of her gorgeous mouth. Then I asked, "Why?"

Kaia's head snapped in my direction, and the expression she wore was filled with the horror she claimed she felt.

"I cried like a baby before falling asleep on you and trapping you," she declared, telling me something I already knew.

"I can think of worse things I've had to endure than having a beautiful woman fall asleep on me," I returned, hoping to ease her mind. It helped a bit but not enough. So, I added, "And I wasn't exactly trapped, Kaia. I think, if I really wanted to, I could have gotten up and left."

She let out a small laugh.

Because I wanted to make sure she didn't feel any shame about what happened and what she'd been through,

I continued, "And anybody else in your position would have cried, too. What you went through was traumatic. It was bound to make you emotional."

Acceptance washed over her, and her features softened entirely.

Damn, she was breathtaking.

"Thank you for being here for me last night," she said softly.

I returned a smile and insisted, "Any time."

"Can I make you breakfast as a way to show my appreciation?" she asked.

I had another idea in mind of how she could show her appreciation but kept that to myself. I didn't think it'd fit in very well with my desire to remain in her good graces.

And because I wanted more time with her in a way that she'd be able to focus on me instead of slaving over the stove, I offered, "How about you let me take you out for breakfast this morning?"

Her brows pulled together, and confusion washed over her. "If you take me out, that's not going to give me the opportunity to show my appreciation," she noted.

"Yes, it is," I assured her.

"How so?"

"I've wanted to take you out since the first day you walked into Archer Tactical," I shared. "This is the perfect opportunity to make that happen."

Kaia's lips parted in shock. Honestly, it surprised me that she felt such astonishment at my admission. I didn't think I'd been doing that stellar of a job hiding the fact that I was attracted to her.

Then again, maybe Kaia was so lost in what was

happening in her own world that she couldn't see what was standing right in front of her.

Of course, now that I knew how recent her heartbreak had been, I'd have to take things slow with her. She deserved that, and quite frankly, so did I. The last thing I wanted was to rush her into something she wasn't ready for and have her realize after we shared far more than we did last night that she'd made a mistake.

I'd do anything to make sure she never thought of me as a mistake, but I still didn't know the full extent of her mindset. I was more than prepared to take the time necessary to figure that out and find a way to reassure her that I was a good guy she could trust.

The only way that could happen was by spending more time with her.

So, taking her out for breakfast was the first step.

"Well, I'm not sure I agree that this is a way for me to thank you for being so kind, but I'm hungry, so I guess I'll let you feed me," Kaia finally replied.

I grinned at her.

"Can you just give me a few minutes to make myself decent?" she asked.

I thought she already looked beautiful.

"Sure," I answered. "Do you mind if I use your bathroom?"

She shook her head and stood up. I followed her through her apartment to the bathroom. She left me there to do my thing while she took off to get herself ready. After I finished up, I returned to the main living space where I'd spent the night with her and waited.

Surprisingly, it didn't take Kaia long to get ready, and

before I knew it, I had her sitting beside me as I drove us to breakfast.

When we were finally seated in a booth at a local diner and had given our breakfast order to the waitress, I asked, "So, now that you've had a minute to wake up and clear your head, how are you really feeling?"

Nodding, she replied, "I'm good, Remi. Honestly. Thank you so much for not making me feel like a basket case. I promise I'm not going to freak out again and lose my mind."

"Kaia, it's okay," I maintained. "I don't think badly at all about how you reacted last night. It was a lot of stuff. In fact, I thought you handled it really well."

"Are you sure you wouldn't lie to me just so I don't feel bad?" she asked.

After letting out a laugh, I answered, "I might, but in this situation, I'm not."

The silence stretched between us for a moment. It wasn't awkward or anything; it was simply there.

I wasn't sure there was a good way to bring up what I wanted to discuss with her, so I decided it was best to just go for it.

"Kaia, listen, I have some things I wanted to talk to you about regarding what you shared with me last night," I started.

Before I could continue, Kaia cut me off and pleaded, "Remi, can we please not do this now? I really don't want to talk about me anymore. Just for a little while."

I didn't know how I was supposed to help her if I didn't understand the full scope of her situation. But the way she was looking at me, her eyes practically begging me to honor her request, I knew I was going to have to wait. She'd shared a lot already and needed a bit more time. I wasn't sure how much time I had to wait since I didn't know what I was dealing with, but if nothing else, I could give her what she wanted through breakfast.

Smiling at her, I moved my head up and down and answered, "Sure. What would you like to talk about instead?"

"You."

I felt my brows shoot up as my eyes opened wide. "Me?" I returned. "What about me?"

Kaia shrugged. "I don't know. Honestly, it doesn't matter to me. Just tell me something about you. Anything. I know. How did you end up making the decision to open a business like Archer Tactical?"

"I didn't."

"What?" she asked, clearly confused.

"Archer Tactical was originally opened more than thirty years ago by my father," I started after our waitress had returned with our breakfast and walked away. "I was about a year old at the time. My dad decided to take years of experience as a former patrol officer and SWAT team member and instructor and use it to train not just professionals but civilians as well."

"Wow, really?"

I nodded. "Yep."

"And you just always knew you were going to follow in his footsteps?" Kaia asked as she lifted a piece of toast to her mouth.

"Yeah," I replied after swallowing a bite of my bacon. "There was no doubt whatsoever in my mind that this is what I was going to do. We grew up seeing how my father lived his life, serving others in a way that was meaningful to him. He's seen a lot, and the passion and dedication he had to making sure people could keep themselves safe was inspiring. It still is."

"He's not…" Kaia trailed off.

Shaking my head, I declared, "He's alive and well. Fit as a fiddle and completely of sound mind. He still comes in regularly and goes out training sometimes, but he's mostly retired. He's got three boys running the show, so he can sit back and enjoy his retirement now."

After swallowing a bite of her eggs, she asked, "Will you introduce me to them tomorrow?"

"My brothers?" I questioned her.

"Yeah. I feel like it's well past time that I apologize to them for ignoring them," she reasoned.

I couldn't stop myself from laughing.

"I promise you that they aren't holding a grudge," I said.

"I know. But I still think I'd like to meet them and apologize. It would make me feel better," she shared as she picked up her glass of orange juice.

"If that's what you want, I'll introduce you tomorrow after our training session," I told her.

"Thanks," she returned. Following a brief pause, she stated, "So, you're one of three boys? What are your brothers' names?"

"Well, first, there are four of us," I started. "Three boys, one girl. I'm the oldest. Vaughn is next. Deacon is the youngest of the boys, and Monroe is the baby of the family."

"You have a sister, too?"

"Yep."

"Does she work at Archer Tactical, too?" Kaia asked.

I shook my head and chuckled. "Monroe is a fierce and loyal sister and friend. She'd do anything she could to help someone out, but she's not a fighter. My sister is a dreamer, and she spends her time dancing."

"Dancing?" Kaia repeated, lifting her fork to her mouth.

"She owns her own studio," I clarified, lifting the last piece of toast from my plate. "When music is playing, everything else fades away for her."

Kaia smiled at me. "I think your sister and I would get along really well," she asserted.

I took a moment to consider that and agreed, "I think you're right. By the way, with everything that happened last night, I didn't get a chance to talk to you about it. You're a DJ?"

At that, Kaia's entire face lit up. I'd never seen anything more beautiful in my whole life.

"I am." She beamed at me. "Does that surprise you?" she asked.

Unable to wipe the smile from my face at the sight of her being so happy, I answered honestly, "There's not much about you that doesn't surprise me, Kaia. And I'm finding I like it all more than I thought I would."

"Remi…" She trailed off.

Not wanting to see her get emotional, even if it was for all the right reasons, I urged, "Tell me how you ended up becoming a DJ?"

"Music has always been an escape for me," she started as she sat back in the booth. "Ever since I was little, I have used it to take me somewhere else when I needed to flee reality. And even though I will do it when nobody else is around, I'm well aware of the fact that I'm not a good singer. So, listening to other people singing is how I make my living and fuel my passion."

I narrowed my eyes on her. I wanted to ask her what

reality she needed to escape from when she was younger, but I promised not to turn this breakfast into something that would upset her. So, I kept it light and focused on the other thing that stuck out to me.

"How do you know you're not a good singer?" I asked.

"I have an ear for things that sound good, especially when it comes to music," she replied. "Trust me, I'm not a singer."

I felt the corners of my mouth twitch. The more I was around Kaia, the more I liked her. And I was finding that I didn't care if she had a horrible singing voice. If she sang, I'd listen.

"I think you should sing for me sometime," I goaded her.

Kaia slowly shook her head. "I'm not that big of a fool," she stated. "If I sing, you'll run away and never come back."

I leaned forward, pressing my forearms onto the table, and teased, "I don't think you know me very well if that's what you think I'd do."

"You haven't heard my singing," she countered. "Trust me on this one. It'd make your ears bleed."

I couldn't help myself. I burst out laughing. Kaia did the same. It felt good, nearly as good as it felt to wake up with her in my arms this morning.

When we finally settled ourselves down, I said, "So tell me how you ended up with this gig at Club Infinity."

Kaia didn't hesitate. She dove in and told me all about how she landed her dream job.

I listened intently, wanting to scoop up every ounce of her I could get.

Suffice to say that even after she finished, I still felt like I hadn't had enough.

CHAPTER 10

Kaia

THERE MIGHT NOT HAVE BEEN A CASTLE IN SIGHT, AND I was certainly no princess, but I felt like I was living in a fairy tale.

It was Monday morning, and I was getting ready to leave for my self-defense training lessons with Remi.

Remi.

That man had been consuming nearly every thought in my mind. I felt like I'd had my head in the clouds for the last twenty-four hours. It was probably a bit longer than that considering it all started when he walked into my DJ booth at Club Infinity on Saturday night.

With the exception of my mini-meltdown when I told him about what had happened with Nolan, everything had been wonderful. I was convinced there was no better man in the world than Remi. He was most certainly the perfect representation of Prince Charming.

And I wasn't even sure he was trying to be that. He just simply was.

That made him even more desirable.

I huffed.

Desire. I hadn't felt desire like this in years. Hell, I wasn't even sure it had felt like this ever.

The way the man spoke, how he treated me, and even the way he ate his food was all so sexy. It was a wonder I could make it through breakfast without having to fan myself.

So, I was feeling great. Fantastic.

The only thing that upset me about where I was right now in my life was the fact that I wanted, more than anything else, to tell Parker about Remi, and I couldn't. Telling her about Remi meant telling her about Nolan. And since lying to Parker about why things ended between Nolan and me wasn't an option, I had to refrain from telling her about Remi. I didn't want to do anything that would distract her from what all of her focus needed to be on.

On the bright side, it didn't feel so bad just yet. For the most part, Parker and I had spent our days communicating mostly via text message since I'd returned from Rising Sun. With Parker's preoccupation with Wren, it just made things easier for her. And I never wanted to call and risk waking my darling niece. But I lived for the daily picture updates Parker sent to me of Wren. She was the most beautiful baby in the world, and I didn't know if I could love her more if I tried.

Since I wanted to focus on the good and remain in fantasyland for just a bit longer, I pushed the negative thoughts about not being able to share with my sister right now from my mind and focused on the good.

Like the fact that I was ready to leave so I could go to Archer Tactical.

I was going to see Remi.

I was going to meet his brothers.

It was going to be a great day.

On that thought, I grabbed my phone and my water and tossed them in my purse. Then I grabbed my keys and left.

What I failed to keep in mind was the fact that in every fairy tale, there's always a villain. I should have remembered and remained cautious, but I didn't. I was too determined to be happy.

And that was my mistake.

Because as I walked from the apartment building toward my car, I heard a familiar voice call my name.

Nolan.

Ignoring him, I continued to move toward my car with a heightened sense of awareness and a quickened pace.

My determination to get away without having any interaction with him was quickly challenged. I started to jog and heard his footsteps pounding on the pavement behind me. I moved faster and shouted, "Leave me alone!"

When I finally made it to the hood of my car, I spun around and repeated myself. My voice firm, I shouted, "Leave me alone."

As I started to back up to the door, Nolan lunged forward and tackled me to the ground. My hands came out to brace for the fall, and tiny rocks scraped at and dug into the skin of my palms.

No.

No. No. No!

Nolan fell at the same time, but he didn't land on top of me. His hands had just barely reached my calves. I kicked them away and scrambled to my feet again, belatedly realizing

I dropped my keys when I fell. Spotting them, I turned back to keep my attention focused on Nolan.

He was advancing. I backed up and shouted, "Go away. I don't want to talk to you."

"We need to talk."

"Leave me alone."

"Kaia, we are going to talk," he insisted.

I needed my keys. I needed my keys, and I needed to get out of here.

I stumbled and nearly fell backward in my haste to retreat, but Nolan reached out and grabbed my wrist. The moment I was steady on my feet again, I pulled my arm away. He let go and captured me from behind.

In an instant, I spun around with my elbow up high and barreled it right into his face. He immediately let me go and put his hands up to cover his face. I didn't stop. I brought my hands to his neck and shoulder, lifted my leg, and kicked him in the groin.

He shouted in agony and dropped to his knees.

For a brief moment, I stood there, completely stunned by what I'd done. I just took him down.

Holy. Shit.

It worked. I did it. Like it was second nature to me, I just did it.

"*You bitch!*" Nolan shouted.

My shock lasted only those few seconds because the second I heard him shout, I realized he was trying to find a way to get back to his feet.

Disengage and get away.

Remi's words rang in my head.

Get away.

110

I needed to go.

Hopping over Nolan, running on adrenaline, I bent down and snatched up my keys. Seconds later, I was in my car with the doors locked and pulling away.

I glanced up in my rearview mirror and saw he had just gotten to his feet as I turned out of the lot with a smile on my face and headed toward Archer Tactical.

My happy mood didn't last long.

As I drove, it started to hit me what had just happened. Though Nolan had kept his previous attacks in the confines of my apartment, it seemed he didn't have any concern about coming after me in broad daylight. He was getting more daring, and I wasn't sure I liked what that could mean moving forward.

After more than two weeks without any contact from him, I had started to let my guard down. I genuinely started to believe he had given up and realized it wasn't worth the effort of coming after me any longer. Apparently, I'd been wrong.

By the time I'd made it to my destination, I'd worked myself up into a frenzy. Maybe it was the sight of the blood pouring from my hands, the fact that the adrenaline had worn off, the fact that I realized Nolan wasn't going anywhere anytime soon, or a combination of all of that. All I knew was I needed to get inside.

I threw my door open and ran across the mostly empty lot to the entrance. There was one thing on my mind. Get to Remi.

I flung the door open with such force; I looked back to make sure it was going to close. But I never stopped moving forward, and that was when I collided with something solid.

Hands gripped my arms firmly as an unfamiliar voice said, "Whoa. Are you okay?"

My eyes shifted to the man I knew was one of Remi's brothers, who was looking down at me with concern in his face as he took in my panicked state.

"Where's Remi?" I demanded.

Confusion replaced the concern before his eyes dropped to my hands and took in the sight of the blood on them.

The next thing I knew, I was being hurried away from the door and back through the space to where I typically found Remi.

"Vaughn, get Remi," the man I now knew had to be Deacon ordered to the other man in the room. "Meet us in the break room."

Vaughn took off in the opposite direction to get Remi while Deacon led me to the break room.

"What happened?" he asked when we came to a stop inside the room.

I glanced down and noticed that a substantial amount of the blood from my hands had ended up on my white T-shirt. I must have looked like I walked right out of a horror film.

Before I could answer Deacon, Remi rushed in. He came to an abrupt halt when he saw me.

My eyes never left him as he scanned me from top to toe.

"Kaia," he rasped as he finally started moving again and came toward me. Once he stopped in front of me, he asked, "What happened?"

"It worked," I declared.

"It worked?" he repeated. "What worked?"

"Everything you taught me," I explained.

Something washed over him, and he put a hand to my

shoulder as he pulled out a chair. "Sweetheart, sit down," he urged.

Sweetheart.

I had a guy I gave a year of my life to who had already beat me up twice and attempted to do it a third time, and I had Remi, a guy who barely knew me and took better care of me than Nolan ever did.

I sat down.

Remi sat down across from me.

Vaughn and Deacon remained in the room.

"Tell me what happened," he encouraged gently.

"I was on my way here," I started. "I walked out of my apartment and was heading to my car. I heard him call my name. It was Nolan. I tried to ignore him, but he kept coming toward me. So, I shouted at him to leave me alone and go away, but he didn't listen. He dove at me just as I reached my car." I held my hands up between us, my palms facing him. "That's how this happened. Anyway, he fell, too. So, I kicked at him, got back up, and realized I dropped my keys. He was back on his feet. I started retreating but almost fell backward. He caught my wrist; I yanked it away. Then he grabbed me from behind, so I did what you taught me. I spun around and elbowed him in the face before I kicked him in the balls. Then I got in my car and drove here."

A look of pride washed over Remi's face. He opened up the first aid kit that Vaughn had placed on the table and immediately started tending to my hands. While he worked, he asked, "Was that everything?"

I nodded. Then I stopped and said, "No. There was one thing I did wrong."

"Baby, you're here, and you're safe, so you didn't do anything wrong," Remi assured me.

I tried to ignore the fact that he called me baby and shared, "But I stood there."

"What do you mean?"

"It was the first time I'd ever done that," I told him. "After Nolan took the kick to his balls, he dropped to his knees. It felt so good to see that. I just froze on the spot and watched him try to breathe through the pain. I was so proud of myself."

The moment I stopped speaking, Remi grinned at me. He glanced to the side where his brothers were standing and said, "Guys, meet Kaia. Kaia, this is Deacon, and this is Vaughn."

I held my free hand up, waved, and said, "It's nice to meet you both." My eyes slid to Deacon's, and I added, "Sorry about nearly knocking you over when I ran in here."

He chuckled and returned, "You're good. Don't worry about it."

"Vaughn, can you call the police, please?" Remi asked.

"I was just about to suggest that," Vaughn replied.

"Police?" I said.

"Yeah."

"You can't do that," I insisted.

Three sets of eyes came to me, but it was Remi who asked, "Why not?"

"Lots of reasons," I returned. "First, they aren't going to do anything. Second, I beat Nolan up. And third, I told him I wouldn't."

"I don't give a shit what you told him you wouldn't do, Kaia," Remi shot back. "This is the third time he attacked you."

"Yeah, and I handled it," I reminded him.

"You might not be so lucky next time," he clipped.

I gasped.

"Fuck, Kaia. I'm sorry. I just… this doesn't make any sense. You need to file a report," he insisted.

I closed my eyes and turned my head away from him.

"Kaia, look at me," Remi urged. His voice was back to being soft and sweet, and I was a sucker for that. When he had my attention again, he asked, "Why would you ever tell him that you wouldn't go to the police?"

My emotions were all over the place, so the minute he asked me that question, I felt my throat get tight. "He had a knife against my throat, Remi."

"Fuck," Deacon hissed. At the same time, Vaughn clipped, "Damn it."

"He's not going to have the chance to do that again," Remi promised.

"He wants to destroy my career," I told him. "I can't… if I go to the police, he's going to go after my job."

"How would he do that?"

"He knows the owner of the club," I explained. "You know, I told you yesterday how hard I worked to get that position. I don't want to lose my job."

Remi tilted his head to the side. He didn't say a word, but there was no missing the clear communication between him and his brothers. With a downward jerk of his chin, Deacon seemed to understand what Remi wanted and walked out. Vaughn said, "I'll wait for him to make his call. Then I'll make mine."

"Thanks, Vaughn."

With that, Vaughn followed Deacon out of the room and left me alone with Remi.

"What's happening?" I asked.

"Deacon is going to call Juan. He's going to fill him in on what just happened to make sure he's aware of it. Then he's going to call the owner of Club Infinity and fill him in on what just happened and confirm that your position at the club isn't going to be affected by this asshole ex-boyfriend. After he does all of that, Vaughn is going to call the police."

"Why would Matt listen to Deacon?" I asked.

Matt was the owner of Club Infinity.

"Because Deacon has known Matt since we were kids," Remi shared. "They were in the same grade from elementary school all the way up through their senior year in high school. They might not have spoken in years, but that doesn't mean they don't respect one another. You have nothing to worry about."

I nodded because… well, what else could I do?

"Now, let me clean up your hands," he urged.

"Are we still going to train today?" I asked.

"Kaia, you got into an altercation today, and you've gotten injured," he noted. "I think it might be best to take a break."

"I had a feeling you were going to say that," I mumbled.

He let out a laugh and continued to work on my hands. When he finished up a few minutes later, he asked, "Are you sure you're okay?"

"Yeah."

Remi sent a sweet smile my way and brought his hand up to cup the side of my face. As his thumb stroked along my cheek, he said, "I'm so proud of you."

I couldn't help myself. I leaned my hand into his touch and whispered, "And I'm so grateful for you."

His hand stilled on my face, and his fingers pressed in. "I need to ask you a question, Kaia."

My lungs stopped functioning because there was something about how he spoke that told me this was serious.

"O… Okay?" I replied.

"I want to know that you're safe," he began. "And I can't do that if I'm away from you. Until we know that this situation with your ex has been handled, I'd like for you to let me take care of you."

"What do you mean?" I asked.

"I think it's a good idea for you to move in with me for just a little while," Remi said.

I blinked in surprise. "Move in with you?"

Nodding, he confirmed, "Yes. I've got a spare bedroom. But if you really don't want to leave your space, I'm happy to go there. I'll take the couch. I just need to know that you're going to be safe."

"Remi… that's… that's a lot," I pointed out. "You can't take this on your shoulders."

"Kaia, I know what I can handle. More importantly, I know what I can't handle. And you being in danger isn't something I can handle," he shared. "Please let me do this. I'll do whatever you need me to do to make you comfortable with this. I promise. You can talk to the police when they get here. They know I'm a good guy. I swear you have nothing to worry about if you agree to this."

I thought about his request for a few moments. It killed me to hear such anguish in his voice. He was genuinely concerned about my well-being.

"I'm not talking to the police about this," I finally told him.

"Kaia, please listen—"

I cut him off and said, "I'm not talking to the police about

117

the kind of guy you are because I think I already know, Remi. I trust you, and I feel safe with you. Why do you think I came here today to begin with?"

He dropped his head, and the tension left his body.

Maybe I didn't realize just how much this was weighing on him.

"Thank you," I said softly.

"For what?"

"For being a good guy."

Remi stood up and held his hand out to me. I took it and lifted myself out of the seat.

"Thank you for trusting me with this, Kaia. It means a lot."

I smiled at him. He curled his arm around my back to my opposite shoulder and gave me a squeeze.

That's when Vaughn popped his head in the room and announced, "Police will be here in five."

"Thanks," Remi responded.

Vaughn jerked his chin up and walked away. Remi looked down at me. "You ready?" he asked.

"Yeah."

"Let's go."

So, that's what I did.

Even if he didn't know I was thinking it, I walked beside my Prince Charming and entered fantasyland again.

What could I say? It was a beautiful place to be.

CHAPTER 11

Kaia

"**T**HANK YOU, OFFICER."

"You're welcome, Ms. Banks. We'll keep you updated."

At that, the officer turned and walked out of the building. I was still at Archer Tactical, and Remi hadn't left my side since he first walked into the room earlier and took care of my hands.

From the moment the police arrived, I'd done nothing but answer questions and recount the details of everything that had happened with Nolan since the first time he'd put his hands on me. After answering even more questions, I found myself surprised by what happened. The officers didn't hesitate to spring into action.

Given my childhood, I hadn't ever seen this happen. To say I was shocked to see how seriously they were taking this would have been an understatement. One of the officers had immediately filed for an EPO, an Emergency Protection Order. An EPO was essentially a restraining order that was effective immediately, but it would only last for seven days. The purpose of the EPO was to offer me instant protection while giving me enough time to get to court so I could file for the temporary order. The EPO was the only way to guarantee that Nolan would face criminal charges if he tried to approach me.

Once I got to the court and had a temporary order in place, it would serve as my protection until a permanent one could be issued. That wouldn't happen for a few weeks until it went through the court process.

Needless to say, I was feeling much better about the whole situation now, and it was all thanks to Remi.

"How are you feeling?" he asked, his voice breaking into my thoughts.

I smiled at him and answered, "I'm good. Thank you for being here for me."

"Anything you need," he promised. His eyes searched my face for a moment before he asked, "So, what do you want to do today?"

"I guess… well, um, do you still think I need to stay with you now that I've got the protection order in place?" I asked.

Remi nodded. "Yes. There is no guarantee that someone like your ex will abide by the rules of the order, so I don't think it's wise to take any chances."

"Okay. So, maybe I should head home and pack up a few things I'll need," I decided.

"I'll take you," Remi declared. "We can stop and grab some lunch while we're out, too."

Remi wanted to take me out for lunch. I knew it wasn't an official date or anything like that, but that didn't mean I didn't like the idea of having time alone with him like that.

And even though I probably should have refused him leaving work to take me home and deal with my mess, I didn't. I wasn't sure I would have won the argument anyway.

"I should talk to Clara, too."

"Who?"

"My neighbor," I explained. "She's the one who tried to intervene the night Nolan attacked me inside the apartment."

Nodding his understanding, Remi said, "Alright. So, I'll take you back to your place so you can pack up a bag and talk to your neighbor. Then I'll take you out for lunch."

So easy. He made everything so easy.

I couldn't help myself. I moved forward, wrapped my arms around him, and said, "Thank you, Remi."

Remi hugged me back. "You're welcome."

We both held on to each other a bit longer before we separated and moved to leave. If I was completely honest, I could have stayed standing there in his arms all morning.

"You seem preoccupied."

That was certainly one way to put it.

I was with Remi at his place, and I was sitting on the opposite end of the couch from him, clutching my phone in my hand.

There was an overwhelming urge inside me to pick up the phone and make one call. Just one call. But I couldn't. I simply couldn't do it.

And the reality of it was settling heavily on my shoulders.

So, as observant as he was and had trained all his life to be, it was no surprise to me that Remi noticed my downtrodden mood.

We had finished eating dinner together, a dinner he cooked, not too long ago. Since it was still too early for bed, he asked if I wanted to just relax and watch some television or a movie. It honestly didn't matter to me, and that's how I knew something much bigger than the day's events was bothering me.

Because being at Remi's house for the first time and having him offer to cuddle up on the couch to watch a movie should have had me feeling all kinds of excitement.

Of course, that wasn't to say that I wasn't appreciative of everything he'd done for me today. It was just that I was finding it hard to feel happy when something was bothering me so much.

Since I couldn't pick up the phone and call the person I wanted to call and Remi was offering a listening ear, I decided to take him up on it.

But because I took too long to come to that decision, Remi had drawn his own conclusions about the cause of my mood. He didn't hold back from sharing it.

"I'm here for you if you want to talk about whatever you're feeling, Kaia," he started. "I know you're probably feeling a lot of emotions over everything that happened today. It might help you deal with it if you take some time to get it out. I promise you've got a safe place to unload those feelings with me."

I offered him a smile. He was such a good guy and a decent human being.

"I appreciate that, Remi," I replied. "And while today has certainly been a challenging day, it's not really the specifics of what happened that are weighing on my mind."

"What's going on?" he wondered.

"I've just been thinking a lot today about my sister and how much I miss her," I shared.

"How did she handle the news?" he asked.

I gave him a questioning look and repeated, "News?"

Nodding, he clarified, "Yeah. I remember you taking a call from her earlier today. How did she react when you told her what happened this morning?"

"I didn't tell her," I confessed. "She doesn't know anything happened. In fact, she doesn't even know that Nolan and I aren't together anymore."

Something washed over Remi's face, but I couldn't read his expression.

"Why wouldn't you tell her?" he questioned me.

His tone was still as gentle as always, even if it was clear that he didn't think my decision made any sense.

"Two reasons," I returned. I opened my phone, tapped on the screen a few times, and found what I was looking for. Then I held it out to him and said, "This is the biggest and most important reason."

As Remi took the phone from my hand to look at the photo, his features softened, and a smile formed on his face. "This is your niece?" he asked.

"That's Wren," I declared, feeling my mood instantly brightened. The little girl was a miracle; the simple thought of her could lift anyone's spirits.

"She's adorable," he said. "And I'm guessing that because she's clearly a very new baby, you're worried that your sister will be preoccupied with your news and not have her attention on Wren. Would that be correct?"

"Observant as ever," I returned.

Remi chuckled.

"Wren is only a few weeks old," I explained. "Just over a month old. I don't want Parker having to worry about anything other than taking care of that little girl."

Nodding his understanding, Remi replied, "Okay. Well, before I give you my thoughts on that, why don't you tell me the rest of it?"

"What do you mean?"

"You said there were two reasons you didn't want to tell your sister about what happened today or the fact that you're no longer in a relationship," he reminded me. "What's the second reason?"

This was not going to be nearly as easy to share as the gorgeous picture of Wren had been. Even still, I knew I wanted to share it. I didn't want Remi thinking I was some crazy girl who made up ridiculous scenarios in her head. More than that, I wanted him to know this truth. I wasn't exactly sure why considering it wasn't something I had even shared with Nolan in all the time that we were together. The fact was that I never really liked to think about it much. I didn't want to focus on it.

But Remi was different.

Something about him made me want to share it.

So, I took in a deep breath and blew it out before I explained, "Parker is the world's best big sister. And after everything the two of us have been through over the years, I want nothing more than for her to live her life feeling nothing but happiness. This will crush her. Not only that, she'll worry so much about me and want to do whatever she could to make sure I was safe."

"Okay, so don't you think that sharing what happened a couple weeks ago and this morning and then explaining how you were able to defend yourself might give Parker the reassurance that she needs to know that you're okay. Wouldn't it help her to know that you've been taking the steps necessary to see to your own safety?"

"Of course it would help, but it would never change who Parker is to me," I countered.

"Why should it?" he asked.

Shaking my head, I said, "Because Parker feels like it's her job to protect me. That's how she's always felt. She's my big sister, and she takes that job seriously. I mean, you're the oldest sibling. I guess it's obvious your brothers can take care of themselves, but I haven't met your sister. If you thought she was in trouble, even if she insisted she had everything under control and knew what she was doing, would you just accept that?"

It was at that question that I think Remi thought he fully understood the reasoning behind my need to keep this whole situation from Parker.

"That very thing happened once with Monroe," he shared. I watched as he ran through something in his mind, likely recalling that scenario with his sister. Then he continued, "And you're right, we didn't sit back and do nothing when we thought she needed our help. As it turned out, she was right and had it handled. But like you said, that didn't change who Deacon, Vaughn, and I are to her, or more importantly, who she is to us. There isn't anything we wouldn't do to protect her."

While I was happy he was finally seeing it from my perspective, he still needed the full truth.

"Parker is the same way," I told him. "She's been my protector since we were kids."

"I think that's normal for older siblings," Remi reasoned.

"Maybe, but Parker is different," I insisted.

"How so?"

I bit the inside of my cheek as I prepared myself to share the truth. Remi didn't miss it, and I think he realized I was about to share something significant.

A moment later, with the soles of my feet pressed to the cushion of the couch and my arms wrapped around my shins, I answered, "My mother died when I was born, and Parker and I grew up with an abusive father."

I wanted to acknowledge the change I saw come over Remi, but I knew if I didn't keep going, I wouldn't be able to get it all out.

So, I continued, "No matter what happened, no matter what he was angry about, Parker's only concern was me. On more than one occasion, I watched my sister put herself in the line of fire for me. Three times he beat me. Three. Parker wouldn't stand for it, so she'd sacrifice herself. She did it over and over. It happened so many times, I lost count. I won't let her do it again."

"Kaia…" Remi trailed off, his voice revealing just how hard he was taking this news.

"We're here now, Remi," I assured him. "Parker and I, despite all that we went through, we're here. We're alive. And she's happy. I'm happy for her. I don't want to take that away from her."

Nodding slowly at me, I could see Remi finally fully understood why it had to be this way. I knew he would. He was a levelheaded guy. He was also the sweetest, which he proved only moments later.

Holding his arm out and open to me, he urged, "Come here, sweetheart."

I couldn't stop myself.

No, that's not right.

I could stop myself.

I just didn't want to.

So, I crawled across the couch, cuddled up next to him, and draped one of my arms across his abdomen while pressing my cheek into his chest. His arm came around me, and when his hand landed on my opposite shoulder, he gave me a gentle squeeze.

It wasn't until I was there, tucked safely into his side, that I realized how much I needed what he was offering. It was also at that point when I finally felt like I could breathe a sigh of relief. I'd finally told someone about what Parker and I experienced as kids, and I had no doubt the reason I was able to let it go had everything to do with the man holding me close.

"How about a comedy?" he asked.

I tipped my head back and looked up at him. "Can you handle a romantic comedy?" I asked.

Remi held the remote out to me and sighed, "Do you have to look at me like that?"

"Like what?" I returned.

"Like I could make all your hopes and dreams come true if I honor this one simple request," he answered.

I wanted to tell him I had a feeling he was already well on his way to making my hopes and dreams come true and that it wouldn't have mattered what we watched. But I didn't share that. Instead, I played along and remarked, "I'm a simple girl, really. It doesn't take much to please me."

Remi's eyes heated, and I realized what I'd just implied.

I quickly looked away and flipped through to find a movie. I hadn't yet found one when Remi announced, "You're the strongest woman I've ever met."

I stopped searching for a movie and looked up at him again.

He smiled at me, and I said, "Just wait until you meet Parker."

Remi considered my words, and something came over him. I didn't have a chance at guessing what that look was until he asked, "So you want me to meet your sister?"

"Sure. Why not?"

"No reason," he replied, a smile tugging at the corners of his mouth. "I have one question, though."

"What's that?"

"Do you realize how incredibly tough you are?" he asked.

I had one encounter that led me to taking a man down to his knees. I hardly thought that qualified me as being *incredibly* tough. But I was too curious to hear Remi's reason, so I countered, "What makes you say that?"

"I don't know everything you've been through in your life, but knowing how you grew up and what you've endured at the hands of your ex, I can't help from feeling like you don't even realize your own strength," he offered.

"Remi, I was never strong," I argued. "With the exception of what happened today with Nolan, I never got away or fought back in a way that kept me from being hurt."

Shaking his head, he declared, "But the physical interactions aren't what make me believe you're strong."

"You've lost me," I said.

"You already said it yourself," he started. "You're here. And I know you meant that in the general sense of being here at this point in your life. I mean it in the sense of you being here right now with me."

That did little to help me understand what he was getting at. Remi realized I was still confused and explained, "Kaia, from everything I learned about you today and what you've gone through, you'd have every reason not to trust me. You'd have every reason not to trust any man, especially when your own father took his hands to you and your sister. But that's not who you are. How do you not realize how strong it makes you that you're open and determined to see the good in other men? You're willing to give them the benefit of the doubt. You're willing to trust them. You're willing to trust me. I feel so lucky that you are who you are and are willing to give me that shot."

I never looked at being strong or tough as anything more than winning in a physical altercation. But Remi made me see that maybe there was a lot more to it than I initially thought. And I loved that he saw me that way.

Warmth spread through me, and my arm tightened across his abdomen. Then I said, "I know good guys exist, Remi. I've never believed that because one man was bad that they were all bad. And I never wanted to punish one man because of something another man had done. I don't want to dwell on the bad things that have happened in my life. I know there is good out there, and I want to find it. My sister did. I see a good man in her husband, Nash. He'd do anything for her and their daughter. And I see a good man in you. Unless you prove to me otherwise, I'm going to believe that what you're showing me is who you really are."

Remi stared at me in silence for a long time. There was a

bit of surprise on his face and tension in his body. He hadn't been expecting that response, but I was glad I gave it to him.

After it settled inside him, the shock was eventually replaced by something else that looked a lot like pride. And a moment later, his thumb began stroking the skin on my shoulder as his body relaxed completely beside mine.

I returned my attention to the television, found a movie I thought he could tolerate, and cuddled closer.

There was no doubt in my mind.

Remi was a good man, and the way I saw it, I was the lucky one.

CHAPTER 12

Kaia

"Excellent job today."

That came from Remi.

I turned and looked back at him. "Thank you. I'm feeling much more confident now than I did a couple of weeks ago," I told him.

"That's a good thing, and it's only going to improve from this point forward. I'm really proud of your progress and impressed with how well you've done," he shared.

"What can I say? I had an excellent teacher."

Remi followed me to the door since our session had ended. Just like he'd done every day since he'd learned about what had happened to me, I knew he'd walk by my side all the way out of the building and to my car.

As we made our way to the front door, I said, "Hey, um, I was wondering what you'd prefer."

"Regarding what?" he asked.

"White rice or macaroni salad with dinner?"

"What's it being served with?" he wondered.

"Hawaiian chicken kebabs."

Remi stopped walking, which meant I stopped walking. When I turned my attention to him, he said, "Hawaiian? Does that mean pineapple is included?"

I grinned at him. "Yep."

He tipped his head to the side, thought for a moment, and answered, "White rice."

"Your wish is my command," I joked as we stepped outside and moved through the parking lot.

"You're a goof," he returned through his laughter.

"I know. If I prepare for seven thirty, will that be okay? Tonight isn't one of your later nights, right?"

Remi came to a stop beside my car and shook his head. "Seven thirty is good. That should give me enough time to get home and get showered," he answered.

"Perfect, I'll see you tonight then," I replied as he opened my door for me. Once I was seated inside, I ended, "Have a good day today, Remi."

"You, too, Kaia. I'll see you at home."

With that, he shut my door and waited outside until I had pulled away with a smile on my face.

It had been a week since I had my encounter with Nolan in my apartment complex's parking lot, and physically speaking, I was back to feeling one-hundred-percent. The scrapes on my hands were essentially all healed up, and as I had told Remi, there had been a nice boost to my confidence.

On Friday, I had gone to court to see a judge and was granted a temporary restraining order, or TRO, as they referred to it. The TRO was going to be in place for three weeks until the point at which the hearing would take place. At that point, the plan would be to have the judge issue a permanent restraining order. Even though they called them permanent, that wasn't exactly the best description. The permanent restraining order would be in place for five years, at which point I could apply to have the judge issue a new one.

Thankfully, there hadn't been any attempts by Nolan to reach out to me. It was my hope that he was taking the sudden legal problems to heart and would back off. If he didn't, he'd face criminal charges.

And now, it was Monday, just after my self-defense lessons with Remi, and I was heading to the grocery store before returning to his house. Though I had a smile on my face, part of me was feeling a bit melancholy because tonight would be my last night there.

Remi wasn't kicking me out.

In fact, he didn't even know that tonight was going to be my last night there. My plan was to make dinner for us tonight and talk to him about it then.

The time at his place had been fantastic. I often found myself looking forward to the evening when he would walk through the door after a long day at work. And on the nights that I had to work, it melted my heart that he'd wait up on the couch for me to get back.

Remi had been the perfect gentleman. He offered me safety and security without it ever being overbearing. He didn't tread on me, and I appreciated that he still respected my independence despite the seriousness of the situation I was involved in.

And for the week we'd spent together, we quickly fell into a comfortable routine. There was no expectation on his behalf that I had to make dinner, but when I'd done it, he didn't complain. He'd return the favor in the morning by making breakfast for the both of us.

So, it worked.

Well, the logistics of it all worked.

If that was all that mattered, I'd have continued living with him for as long as he'd have me. But logistics weren't all that it was about.

I couldn't continue to ignore my basic human instincts. Or perhaps they were urges. Remi was everything I could have ever wanted in a man, and each time I saw him, I had to resist the temptation to tear the man's clothes off his perfect body.

I didn't know how much a girl was supposed to take, but I knew I couldn't do it any longer.

Of course, I also didn't want to continue to take advantage of his hospitality. Remi had been more than generous by allowing me to stay with him, but now that the dust had settled and the TRO was in place, I thought it was time to go home.

I just hoped a delicious dinner would offset any adverse reaction he might have had. I wasn't a fool. I knew Remi wasn't going to take this lightly. It simply wasn't in his nature to kick a girl out who had a very volatile threat out there waiting for her.

But this couldn't go on forever. So, I was willing to do whatever I had to do to make it sting a little less.

A couple hours later, about an hour before I expected Remi to return, my phone rang.

My screen lit up with an image of the most beautiful baby in the world being held in her mother's arms, and I instantly smiled.

Parker was calling.

"Hey," I greeted her as I slipped the phone between my

ear and shoulder and wiped my pineapple-juice-covered hands on the dishrag. "How's my favorite baby doing?"

"She's brilliant."

"Of course, she is," I declared. "She takes after her aunt. How are you doing?"

"Well, I'm glad to know I'm second on your list," Parker teased.

"Oh, you know I love you. I just can't help myself when it comes to Wren. I'm sure you understand what that's like. I can't even comprehend how much I love her," I replied.

"I know what you mean. I was just joking with you. And I'm doing okay," she assured me.

I never had any doubt about my sister's ability to be a good mother. She'd practically raised me since I was six and our grandmother died, leaving us with our father as the only adult in our lives.

"Are you getting sleep?" I asked.

"You know, it's not been too bad," she answered. "I mean, she gets up a couple times throughout the night. But as soon as she's been changed and fed, she goes right back to sleep. She's been such a good baby."

"And is Nash adjusting okay to fatherhood?"

I heard my sister sigh, and I already knew what her answer was going to be. Even still, I waited so she could share it with me.

"He's the best man I've ever known, Kaia," she swooned. "He's such a good father, better than I could have ever dreamed of for my child. He's the father I wish we would have had."

It made my heart so happy to hear that. I already knew that Nash was a great guy and would bend over backward for my sister. But to hear Parker tell me that he was all that he should have been and more for Wren just made everything better.

I wanted that. I wanted to have a man I could depend on the way Parker could depend on Nash. I wanted a man who'd one day be a better father to our children than the one I had. I wanted a man who made me feel the way Remi did.

I wanted Remi.

"I'm so happy for you, Parker. You deserve this," I said.

"It's really incredible. I can't wait for you to experience it all, too," she returned. "Speaking of which, how is everything going out there with you?"

"Okay. I've been busy, and work has been great."

"That's good. How's Nolan?" she asked.

Shit.

I didn't want to lie to her.

But I couldn't speak the full truth. Not being so far away from her. That would have to wait until I could see her and tell her to her face. She'd need to see me to know that I really was okay.

Following a delayed silence, I confessed, "Nolan and I are no longer together."

Parker gasped. "What? When did this happen?"

"A few days after I got back from Rising Sun," I admitted.

"Why didn't you tell me? Are you okay?"

This was precisely the reason why I didn't tell her. I could already hear the panic in her tone. She was worried for me. I loved that she cared so much, but I hated knowing what it would do to her.

"I'm fine," I assured her. "I promise. Trust me when I tell you that this was for the best. We never would have worked out in the long run."

"Oh, Kaia, I'm so sorry," she lamented. "Are you sure you're okay?"

"I really am. It's actually been good for me," I insisted. Then, because I didn't want to dwell on this much longer nor did I want her to ask a question that would force me to lie, I added, "In fact, I'm going to be looking into flights back to Rising Sun so I can come to visit again. I know I was just there not too long ago, but I miss you guys."

"Are you really? That'll be so much fun. We miss you, too," she bubbled.

Just like that, I'd turned Parker's mood around. Since I knew there was one thing that would keep her distracted from my situation with Nolan, I didn't hesitate to take advantage.

"So, how much did you tell me Wren weighs now?" I asked, doing my best to sound chipper. If I was being honest, it wasn't hard. Just thinking about that little girl put a smile on my face.

Thankfully, my plan worked out fabulously, and Parker and I spent the rest of our call talking about Wren. By the time we disconnected, I only had a few minutes left before Remi was going to be back. So, I finished prepping the food and thought about my sister.

A little while later, I was out on Remi's deck waiting for the grill to heat up when the door slid open, and he walked out.

"Hey," he greeted me with a smile on his face.

Even though I wasn't feeling thrilled, I returned the smile and greeting. "Hey."

"Are you okay?" he asked.

I should have known he was going to figure me out. I

wasn't okay, but I didn't want to risk ruining dinner because we got into a conversation too soon.

"I just have some things on my mind," I answered.

"Do you want to talk about them?"

"We can talk after dinner," I told him.

He gave me an assessing look. "Are you sure?"

Not wanting him to worry, I said, "I promise."

With my vow, Remi let it go and asked, "Do I have time to shower?"

"Yeah, you've probably got twenty to twenty-five minutes before the food is ready," I said.

"Okay, I'll be back then."

At that, Remi turned and walked away. My eyes stayed on his ass until he disappeared inside.

Twenty-five minutes later, while we were seated out on his deck on the gorgeous summer evening, Remi declared, "Hawaiian chicken kebabs are my new favorite food."

"Are you just saying that so I'll make them again for you sometime?" I asked.

"Yes. But I'm also saying it because it's the truth."

"Thank you."

For a few minutes, the two of us ate together in comfortable silence, thoroughly enjoying the food and the company. Before too long, I asked him about his day at work, and he filled me in on it.

And the next thing I knew, we'd finished eating, and Remi was done waiting.

"So, what's on your mind?"

"Just a couple of things," I answered. "There's one thing, in particular, that I wanted to talk to you about."

"Okay. What is it?"

"Tonight is going to be my last night here," I announced.

Confusion marred Remi's features. "Why?" he asked.

"Well..." I trailed off, trying to think of how to best phrase it. When everything I thought I would say flew out the window, I just had to wing it. "Things have had a chance to calm down, and I have the TRO now. I don't think he's going to want to risk criminal charges or jail time just so he can try to talk to me again."

"But he didn't try to contact you immediately after that night he attacked you when you came home from work," Remi noted. "A guy who is willing to put his hands on a woman the way he did to you is not someone whose judgment I'd trust. You and I might realize that having that restraining order is reason enough not to go near someone, but I don't think we should assume he'd see it the same way."

I didn't necessarily disagree with anything he was saying. It was just that I thought it sounded better to tell him that I was feeling confident enough about that situation to be able to return home.

I just wasn't sure that telling him the full truth—that I was insanely attracted to him—was a reason he'd find as acceptable for me to leave.

So, I tried a different tactic. "Remi, I don't want to take advantage of your kindness and generosity," I started. "I really appreciate everything you've done for me, but I don't want to overstay my welcome."

"Did I do something to make you feel like you were putting me out?"

I shook my head. "Oh, no. Absolutely not. You've been... you've been wonderful."

Remi leaned forward and stared intently at me. He

searched my face for a long time, and there was something in his eyes I couldn't read. I certainly didn't have the skills he did for reading people. Maybe that's what I needed to start getting lessons for.

After the silence stretched between us for a long time, his stare unwavering, his voice dipped low, and he insisted, "You don't have to leave, Kaia."

"I know that," I assured him. "I just think maybe it's time I start getting back to normal. I know you're not kicking me out or anything like that."

Gosh, why was this so hard?

"I like having you here," he declared.

What? Was he saying…

"Remi, if this is about the Hawaiian chicken—"

"It's not about the chicken, sweetheart," he cut me off as he scooted his chair closer to mine.

His face was mere inches from mine. His lips were so close. I felt nerves in my belly that I hadn't felt in years.

"What's it about then?" I whispered.

"This."

The next thing I knew, his beautiful mouth touched mine as his hand drove into my hair and cupped me behind the head.

For a moment, my body had gone stiff as I tried to process the fact that Remi was kissing me. Then it hit me that Remi was kissing me, and his tongue had come out to touch my lips.

So, I parted my lips and let him taste me.

Then all the tension that had been running through my body melted away, along with all my thoughts about moving back home.

CHAPTER 13

Remi

I COULDN'T LET HER GO.

All it took was one week.

Seven whole days of having her at my place, seeing her every night, and watching her face light up when I walked into the room. After having that, I couldn't give it up.

I couldn't give her up.

Kaia and I might not have spent every waking moment together, but the time that we did have together was some of the best.

At least once a day, Kaia made me laugh. More than a couple times a day, she smiled at me in a way that I felt in my gut. And every night that we curled up on the couch together after having dinner together, she did it wearing short cotton shorts and tiny tops that I felt in my cock.

And now she wanted to leave?

She wanted to take all of that away from me?

No.

No way could I allow that to happen without at least letting her know how she made me feel.

I knew it was risky. I wasn't sure if she was ready for it, but I had to take my shot. Not only was I terrified of no longer feeling every day the way I felt over the last week, but I was also worried about her leaving.

While I understood her need to believe that everything with her ex was as good as over now that she had the temporary restraining order, I wasn't convinced. I didn't know the guy at all, but I'd met a ton of people like him over the years. If he was anything like the rest, he wasn't through with Kaia. He wasn't just going to walk away without another word. Someone like him didn't think the rules applied to him. So, even though Kaia saw that order as a deterrent, I wasn't convinced this guy did. If he wanted to come after her, a piece of paper wasn't going to stop him, even if it meant he'd face criminal charges or jail time. All too often, people like him thought they'd be able to get away with it. Some did. But I'd be damned if I let him get to her.

I knew it from the moment she first walked into Archer Tactical. The feeling was only solidified when I learned the reality of her situation.

Kaia was mine. Everything I'd spent my entire career training for had brought me to this moment. I'd do anything to protect her.

That's why there really was no other option in my mind. I was going to go for it, hope for the best, and cross my fingers that I could change her mind. This was my first choice and last resort to convince her to stay.

Luckily, and much to my surprise, it only took Kaia a

moment to realize what was happening, give into my kiss, part her mouth, and let me taste her.

It was far better than I could have ever imagined. And that was saying something considering how much imagining I'd done since I first met her.

Her kiss left me feeling excited and hopeful that what was ahead for us would be just as phenomenal. Even if it was half as good as what I was experiencing with her now, it would be stellar.

But based on what I was getting from her now, I didn't think I had to worry about it only being half as good.

Because even though I'd worried that I'd pushed for something she wasn't ready for too soon, I quickly learned I was wrong. Other than those few moments when I first touched my mouth to hers, Kaia didn't hold herself back. The minute she let herself go, she opened up completely.

It was incredible, and I wanted more.

I slipped my arm around her waist and gave her a gentle tug. Kaia's hands flew to my shoulders as I urged her body closer toward mine. The next thing I knew, her gorgeous thighs had straddled my lap, and she was moaning as she began to grind her hips over me.

There was nothing sexier. If she kept it up, if she continued to make those sounds while she moved her body like that, I was worried I'd come in my pants.

Yep.

No doubt about it.

I didn't have to worry about anything that was to come only being half as good as her kiss.

Kaia had already demonstrated that she knew exactly

what she was doing, and she was going to make this the best night of my life.

Keeping one hand planted firmly on her bare thigh, the other drifted down over her ass. As I squeezed her there, I reluctantly tore my mouth away from hers. For a moment, neither of us moved as we stared at one another. The only movement was the rapid rise and fall of Kaia's chest.

That alone would have been enough for me to make that next move, but I waited to bury my face in her chest when she breathed, "Remi."

Fuck.

Hearing her say my name like that, filled with lust and need and desire. I could die a happy man now.

As I kissed her neck and chest, my hands drifted to her hips and up her sides, stopping once my thumbs were just beneath the underside curve of her breasts. I lifted my head again to look at her.

Her eyes were pleading with mine. She wanted this. It was possible, judging by that look in her eyes, that she wanted it even more than I did.

I swiped my thumb up and over her nipples.

A ragged moan escaped from the back of her throat as her body shuddered over mine.

Damn.

For a moment, I was stunned, unable to move. But then it occurred to me that I could see and hear that once more if I found a way to move my thumbs again.

So, I did.

And Kaia moaned again, this one much deeper and huskier.

If I didn't know any better, I'd have thought she was on the verge of an orgasm.

"Remi," she rasped. "Please."

"I want you to sleep in my bed tonight, Kaia," I told her. She rolled her hips, and I groaned.

"Take me there," she begged.

I didn't need any additional instructions or encouragement. Not caring that we were leaving the evidence of our dinner outside on the table on the deck, I stood with Kaia in my arms, keeping her body planted firmly against mine, and carried her inside.

With Kaia's legs around my waist, her ankles hooked behind my back, and her mouth kissing me along my neck while her hands drove into my hair, I made my way through the house toward the bedroom. And I did it wondering if this was a dream.

By the time I made it to my bedroom and placed her in the bed, I decided I didn't care if this was a dream or not. I was going to fully immerse myself in it and enjoy every single second.

The first thing I was going to do was memorize the vision of her in my bed. Even fully clothed, she was sublime.

I reached behind my head, grabbed my T-shirt behind my neck, and quickly removed it. The second it was gone, Kaia moved. She was no longer on her back. Like a flash, she came onto her knees and shifted to the edge of the bed. Then she began exploring.

Her fingertips traced delicately over the skin of my chest and abs while her mouth left no spot untouched. Kaia was so lost in what she was doing, she didn't even look up at me when she murmured, "I've wanted to do this for weeks now."

Weeks? She wanted to do this for weeks?

Why the hell had I held myself back?

The whole time I'd been thinking I was doing the right thing by giving her time, and she never needed or wanted it. And now I was struggling to maintain a modicum of self-control while I relished the feel of her gentle touch on my skin.

"Baby," I rasped, needing to get her attention.

Kaia's fingers pressed in firmly at my sides as her chin tipped up, and she brought her beautiful eyes to mine.

For a moment, I was utterly captivated. I lifted my hand to the side of her face and stroked my thumb along her cheek.

"You're so beautiful," I told her.

She melted.

Right there in front of me, I watched as everything in her body and expression softened. It was as though hearing me say those three little words to her were akin to handing her the whole world. Nobody had ever looked at me the way she did at that moment.

Putting her hands to my shoulders, Kaia lifted up so her face was directly in front of mine. Her eyes searched every feature for a few seconds before she leaned forward and kissed me. My arms immediately went around her.

I couldn't get enough.

I didn't want to stop kissing her, but I also had about a thousand other things I wanted to do to her.

Kaia began rolling her hips forward, communicating to me that she needed more than she was getting. Since I had every intention of giving her everything, I wasted no more time. We tore our mouths from one another as I brought my hands to the hem of her tank and lifted it over her head.

From there, things became a bit more frantic. Before I

knew it, her bra had been tossed aside, and her shorts and underwear had been pulled down her legs. I was naked right alongside her a moment later and climbing into the bed with her.

My body was covering half of hers, my knee planted into the mattress between her thighs. I dropped my mouth to her chest, instantly sucking one of her nipples into my mouth. While my tongue swirled around and flicked over the hardened bud, one of my hands squeezed and played with the opposite breast.

Through it all, Kaia didn't stop squirming and moaning. Her fingernails dug into the skin at the back of my shoulders while she arched her back and sent her tit deeper into my mouth.

Hearing her like this, knowing how desperate she was for more, I couldn't stop myself from groaning.

When I moved my mouth to the other breast, my hand slid down her abdomen to her pussy. One finger swiped through. Kaia's body shuddered again.

Drenched.

Unable to stop myself, I slipped my finger inside her. A guttural moan escaped her, and I had to lift my head from her chest to watch her.

Keeping one hand on her breast, my thumb grazing over her nipple, and my other hand between her legs, I kept my eyes on her face. With each stroke of my finger inside her, Kaia was climbing higher and higher. It had been mere minutes, and she was already there.

Weeks.

She had wanted this for weeks.

And now she was going to have it.

"Remi," she panted.

I slipped a second finger inside and worked her faster. The rise and fall of her chest grew quicker, her breathing becoming shallow. And the moans never stopped.

The sound of her so turned on and close to orgasm was enough to do me in. By some miracle, I managed to hold myself off and focus on giving her every bit of my attention.

And the next thing I knew, Kaia's legs began to tremble as she pressed the back of her head deeper into the mattress. Her fingernails bit harder into my skin as she held on, riding wave after wave of pleasure.

There was nothing more beautiful than looking at and listening to her like this.

When she finally came down from the high, she closed her eyes and smiled. Her fingertips were featherlight on my skin as they traveled down my arms. When they moved back up, they drove into my hair, and she pulled me toward her.

Without wasting a second, Kaia kissed me—deep, intense, and sweet.

Her lips had barely left mine when she demanded, "Fuck me, Remi. Please, fuck me now."

The raspy edge to her voice mixed with her request had me moving quickly. I rolled on a condom, belatedly noticing that Kaia's eyes had drifted shut. But when I settled myself over her again, she brought a hand to the side of my face and dragged her thumb along my bottom lip.

With our eyes locked on one another, I positioned myself and surged forward. Kaia's lips parted as her chin tipped up, exposing her throat.

Fuck, she felt good.

Burying my face in her neck, I kept my hips still. This woman was perfect in every way.

After giving myself a moment to rein in the excitement, I lifted my head again, looked down at her, and pulled my hips back before pushing forward again.

The second stroke was slow, but that's where it ended. All I cared about was delivering every bit of pleasure I could to Kaia from that point forward.

She wanted me to fuck her. I'd fuck her. I'd fuck her so hard she'd wake up tomorrow morning and forget all about her ridiculous idea to leave.

Looking down at her gorgeous body, listening to the sounds of her moans, and feeling the wet warmth of her wrapped around me, I got lost in her.

Completely.

I drove in fast. I drove in hard. I drove in deep.

Then we rolled to our sides, and I hooked her leg over my hip. As I continued with the steady pace of my thrusts, one of my hands gripped her ass firmly. The other was planted in her hair at the back of her head and tugging back gently so I could kiss her throat, her jaw, and her mouth. There wasn't any part of her I didn't want to devour.

"You feel so good, baby," I said, my voice a deep growl.

"Remi," she breathed.

One word was all she could manage. I was glad that one word was my name.

Rolling to my back, I took her with me. And though she might not have been able to formulate a coherent sentence, Kaia did not disappoint when it came to riding my cock.

She did it with enthusiasm. She did it at a pace that was

not the least bit lazy. And she did it in a way that made me never want it to end.

The build-up to her second orgasm was incredible. Just before she was about to go over the edge, I clamped an arm around her waist, planted the other on top of her thigh, and powered my cock into her.

"Oh, God," she whimpered. "Remi."

I moved faster. I drove in harder. I took it deeper.

She went soaring seconds before I did, and I worked us both through to the end.

For a long time afterward, neither of us said anything. Kaia simply stayed on top of me, her thighs on either side of my body as my fingers caressed the heated skin on her back.

It took some time for our breathing to return to normal. When it did, I declared, "I'm not ready for you to move back home yet, Kaia."

There wasn't an ounce of hesitation in her voice when Kaia returned, "Okay, Remi. I'll stay here with you."

After what we just had, I wasn't sure how there was any tension left in my body. But with her promise to stay, I felt like a weight had been lifted off my chest.

I might have tried to make it seem like it was only because I was concerned about her safety, but that couldn't have been further from the truth. I didn't want her to leave because even though it had only been a few weeks since I'd met her, I already knew I was falling for her.

CHAPTER 14

Kaia

"**T**HAT ALL WENT A LOT BETTER THAN I HAD expected."

Remi's arm tightened around me as he chuckled. We were back in his bed following a second round, which started not long after the first had ended. We'd both cleaned up, Remi went downstairs to lock up the house for the night, and now we were here.

While I didn't think either one of us was officially ready to call it a night, there was no question in my mind that we were both in serious need of a small break to recuperate. Or, maybe Remi didn't need a break. I did.

And it shouldn't have come as a surprise, either. I should have known that if things were going to go where they just went between us, Remi would have been nothing less than stellar.

Truthfully, even though I'd seen the way he occasionally looked at me and realized there was some attraction,

I hadn't expected his words after we'd had sex with each other the first time.

He didn't just want me to stay for my safety; he wanted me to stay for him.

I couldn't say no because, well, I didn't want to.

What I'd learned about him from the day I first met him until just before he kissed me was already more than enough for me. The fact that he was all that he was and he was also an incredible lover was the icing on the cake. I almost felt bad that I'd experienced everything that made up Remi Archer. If I had my way, no other woman would ever know what that was like.

Of course, I realized I was getting way ahead of myself. But I couldn't remember a time in my life when I felt this good. Considering I was someone who hadn't had a whole lot of good fortune when it came to men, I wanted to make sure I held on as long as I could.

It wasn't like Remi didn't make it easy. He was strong, confident, handsome, and protective. I could have been happy with just that. But add on the fact that he knew how to make my body feel good and give me precisely what I needed, even when I never opened my mouth to share it, and I was considering myself to be a fortunate woman. His ability to do that—to read me in such an intimate way—was a bit astounding, but I guessed it was one of the perks of his job. It trained him to be that kind of lover. I'd be a fool to be in my position and complain about it.

Which is why I didn't.

Instead, as part of my tactic to give myself a bit of a rest, I did the very opposite of complaining and praised him for a job well done. It seemed he had questions.

"What were you expecting?" he asked.

"A lot," I confessed, lifting my cheek from his bare chest to look at him.

Remi grinned at me before he returned, "Happy to know I was able to exceed your expectations."

"You're an incredible lover, Remi," I declared. "I just…" I trailed off. I wasn't sure if perhaps I was about to share too much.

"What?" he asked, his body going solid beneath mine. "You just what?"

Biting my lip nervously, I considered whether to tell him the full truth. I'd never really been one to hold back, so I ultimately decided this wasn't the time to start. Especially not when the man deserved to hear it.

"If I had known all I needed to do was tell you that I was leaving for you to respond the way that you did, I would have done it a lot sooner than tonight," I admitted.

His fingers on the hand that was resting on my bare ass pressed in a bit before he said, "If I had known you wanted me as badly as you did, I wouldn't have waited so long to kiss you."

"You make it sound like I'm some sex fiend," I retorted.

"Sweetheart, you begged me to fuck you," he reminded me. "Both times."

I did do that. The first time I'd simply been desperate to feel him. The second time I knew what I was going to get and didn't want him to delay in delivering it.

When I took too long to respond because I ended up getting lost in remembering just how wonderful it had been when he honored my request, Remi added, "I loved it."

"What?"

"Everything," he started. "Everything about the way you were, how hungry you were for me, I loved it. You're so sexy, Kaia. And having a woman that looks like you do, kisses the way you do, and begs me to fuck her like you do is all I think I could ever want."

Wow.

Wow. Wow. Wow.

We were only hours into this. We hadn't even discussed what this was; and yet, Remi believed I was all he could ever want.

"Does this seem fast to you?" I asked.

He shrugged. "I don't know. I don't really care, to be honest," he answered. "I like how it feels. I like you, and I like being around you. If I had my way, we would have done this that first weekend after I met you."

My brows shot up in surprise.

"Don't look so shocked," he said. "You know you're beautiful. And funny. And badass. And confident. Why wouldn't I want you?"

I didn't want to cry, but nobody, not one single person other than my sister, had ever said anything like that to me. My emotions were going to get the best of me if I didn't do something about this. So, I gave myself a minute to take a few deep breaths in an effort to stave off the tears.

When I was sure I had it under control, I declared, "I have a confession to make."

"Okay?"

"I never wanted to leave for any of the reasons I gave you earlier tonight," I confessed. "Or, I guess they weren't really the main reason I wanted to go back home."

"So, what was it?" he asked.

"You."

"Me?"

Nodding, I explained, "Yes, you. Remi, do you understand how difficult it has been for me to act like a lady and not jump on you the minute you walk into the room? I was struggling, and it was just getting harder and harder to be around you so often without being able to touch you."

"You touched me before," he pointed out.

I shook my head. "Not the way that I wanted to," I told him. "And I certainly didn't get to kiss you either."

Remi squeezed my ass again and let out another laugh. "Well, I'm glad we worked it out and that you're going to stay."

Smiling at him, I returned, "Me too."

"And I'm even happier that you won't have to hold yourself back from touching me or kissing me in all the ways that you want," he added.

My smile grew, and I agreed, "I'm happy about that, too."

I put my cheek back down on his chest, and a comfortable silence fell across the room. My fingers stroked lazily over Remi's pec while his did the same over my hip and ass. It was nice. Comfortable.

But after some time passed, he asked, "So, what else was it?"

My fingers stopped moving. "What else was what?" I returned.

"Earlier tonight, you told me you had some things on your mind," he began. "We've already dealt with one of those things. I'm wondering what the other things were so that maybe we can work those out for you, too."

"Oh, well, I guess it's just really one other thing," I clarified.

"Okay, so what is it?"

"My sister," I said.

"What about her?"

"I talked to her earlier in the day today," I started. "It was about an hour before you got home. Anyway, I ended up telling her that Nolan and I broke up not long after I got back from my visit with her. I did my best to assure her that I'm okay, but she's still worried. She wants me to be happy, and so, I know she's now thinking I'm suffering from some massive heartbreak."

"Are you?" he asked.

"Not at all," I insisted.

"Did you tell her that?"

"Yes, but she's Parker. She's always going to worry about me. In fact, I think it's going to be even worse now that I'm so far away from her," I explained. "The thing is, I really miss her and the baby. I miss all three of them, to be honest. I want to give her the truth about the whole thing, but I can't do it over the phone. I need her to see me so that when I tell her, she'll be able to see that I'm okay and that I'm happy."

"Maybe you should make plans to go visit her then," Remi suggested.

I lifted my head and stared at him. I wanted to laugh. Nolan detested the time I spent talking about Parker, or more recently, gushing over Wren. And here was Remi, urging me to go visit my sister.

Was this man even real?

"I was kind of already thinking about doing that," I shared.

"That's good. Where does she live anyway?" he asked.

"Surprisingly, despite everything she endured there, Parker never left our hometown. She's living in a small town in Northwestern Wyoming called Rising Sun," I shared.

Remi's whole body went solid.

Even though I felt it, I somehow ignored it and went on, "You've probably never heard of it, but it's not far from the Jackson Hole area."

"I've heard of it," he deadpanned.

"Really?" I asked, feeling surprised that he knew of the location.

Remi nodded and said, "I've actually been there several times."

I tipped my head to the side and pressed, "You have? For what?"

There was a brief hesitation before he answered, "That's where my sister lives."

"You're lying," I accused him.

Remi shook his head. "I'm not. She moved out there years ago after two of her three best friends did," he shared. "Monroe and her other best friend that was still here in California made a couple trips out to visit the other two. While she was there, she met the man she's now married to. Have you ever heard of the professional snowboarder, Xander Stone?"

My mouth dropped open.

"Your sister is married to him?"

"Yep," he confirmed. "And her three best friends are married to his three best friends."

"I can't even believe this," I marveled. "How crazy is this that your sister and my sister both live in Rising Sun?"

"I don't think it's crazy at all," Remi said. "I think it's a great thing."

Wow. Wow. Parker and Monroe both lived in the same city. Remi's sister moved to the town I was raised in while I moved here.

I was dumbfounded.

"Kaia?"

"Yeah?"

"How about you plan a trip to go back to see your sister?" he suggested again. "Let me know when you're going to go, and I'll come with you. I can introduce you to my sister while we're out there."

"You want me to meet her?" I asked.

"Why wouldn't I?" he countered.

"I don't know. Will she be okay with it?" I pressed.

Remi's hand, which had been alternating between squeezing my ass to tracing lazy circles with his fingertips, stopped moving.

"She's going to love you," he insisted. "Not only will she love the fact that you're a DJ, but like I said before, she's a dreamer. She'll love knowing that I've found someone who makes me happy."

And with those words, I was back to thinking that this was moving fast between us. Remi was already so confident about us, and that made me feel good. Nolan and I had been together for nearly a year, and he hadn't introduced me to any of his family. That should have been the first red flag.

"You like me a lot, don't you?" I asked.

"Yes, baby, I do."

"Are we… are we going to be going to Rising Sun as a couple or—"

Before I could finish my question, Remi cut me off and asserted, "We're exploring this between us, Kaia. We're exclusive. From this point forward, we're a couple. Are you good with that?"

I nodded slowly, loving where this was headed. "I'm very good with that."

"Good. Now, how do you feel about kids?"

It was suddenly my turn to have my body go solid. "Remi, we just had sex for the first time tonight," I reminded him, not knowing why that even needed to be said. "I think you're moving a little too quick."

He burst out laughing and rolled me to my back, half of his body covering mine. I couldn't do anything but listen to and feel what his laughter did to me. I loved it a whole lot.

When he finally settled himself down, he clarified, "I wasn't talking about us having kids, sweetheart. I was talking about my sister. She's got four of them. Archer, Harper, Phoenix, and Tessa."

"Wow," I marveled. "How old are they?"

"Five, four, three, and two. Archer is five, Harper is four, Phoenix is three, and Tessa turned two at the beginning of this year."

I blinked up at him. "I'm guessing Monroe likes being pregnant?"

"Her husband didn't have any blood relatives left, and my sister would do anything to make him happy. After Archer was born, they decided they wanted a big family. I'd like to think they're done by now, but who knows," Remi stated.

"I love that she used your family's surname as her son's first name," I remarked. "Parker and Nash named their daughter after his sister, who died when they were just kids. Her name was Wren. They used my name for her middle name, so my niece was named after both of her aunts. And to answer your question, while I'm not quite ready for any of my own just yet, I do love kids. I can't wait to meet your nieces and nephews."

Remi smiled and touched his mouth to mine. That soft kiss quickly led to something much more profound. And just like that, he initiated round three.

I didn't know how it was possible, but it was just as perfect as the first two were.

After we cleaned up and climbed back into his bed, Remi turned out the light and curled his body around the back of mine. He draped his arm over my side and tucked me close to him. Then he pressed a sweet kiss to my bare shoulder.

For a long time, I allowed myself to enjoy how it felt to have him holding me. I started to wish I'd met him sooner. Of course, that led me to thinking about how the only reason I even met him was because I'd been with Nolan first. Then thoughts of Nolan invaded my mind, and I found I couldn't drift.

"Remi?" I called quietly.

"Right here, baby," he returned, his voice so soothing and gentle.

"Do you really think I have to be worried about Nolan doing something crazy?" I asked.

There was a brief pause before Remi answered, "It's not you who has to be worried."

"What does that mean?" I wondered.

"We just discussed what's happening here between us," he began. "We're exploring this. You're mine. If that guy decided to do something crazy, he's the one that's going to need to be worried."

"Why do you say that?" I asked.

"Because I protect what's mine, Kaia."

There was nothing left to be said. Remi protected what was his. I was his. And though I'd been feeling more and more confident about my ability to defend myself in a physical altercation with someone like Nolan, I liked the fact that Remi wanted to be the one to protect me.

On that thought, I cuddled closer and finally found sleep.

CHAPTER 15

Remi

"**Y**OU'LL BE GONE BEFORE I GET BACK?"

"Yeah."

"Are you going to miss me?"

"Yeah."

"Okay, sweetheart, give me a kiss."

Though she had already stepped forward into the space created by the open car door, at my request, Kaia turned and moved close to me. She brought both of her hands up to frame my face, her fingers drifting back slightly into my hair. Then she pressed up on her toes and kissed me.

I had slipped one arm around her waist and pulled her close when she did. Every night since that first night together, Kaia had slept in my bed. Despite that, despite having her tucked close every night as I fell asleep and by my side when I woke up in the morning, I still couldn't get enough of her.

Eventually, we begrudgingly tore our mouths away from one another.

"I should get going," Kaia said. "I've got some phone calls to make."

"Okay. Drive safe."

"Have a good day at work, Remi," she returned.

With that, I held open her door and waited for her to fold in and get herself buckled before I closed her door. Then, even though I started walking back toward the entrance of Archer Tactical, I lingered outside until she had pulled out of the lot.

A moment later, I strode back indoors, prepared to put in a full day of work. But I barely had a minute to start thinking about what was on my schedule for the day when I heard, "Someone is holding out."

I looked up and over to my right to see Deacon and Vaughn were both looking at me with smirks on their faces.

"What?"

Deacon moved forward, put his hand to my shoulder, and squeezed. "I feel wounded, Remi," he started. "We're your brothers."

"Okay. And?"

"And you didn't tell us you and Kaia got serious," he explained. "Or, even if it's not serious, you didn't tell us that things were no longer strictly professional."

I rolled my eyes. "Where are you getting this information?" I asked.

"There's a window," Deacon reminded me. "We just saw you two together out in the parking lot."

I should have guessed that. Well, it seemed there was no time like the present.

"Things changed," I confessed.

"When did this happen?" Vaughn asked as Deacon and I both moved to grab a stool.

"Monday night," I answered. "I got home from work, and Kaia told me after we had dinner together that she wanted to move back to her apartment."

Confusion washed over both of my brothers' faces, but it was Deacon who spoke.

"Okay, I have a lot of things I want to say about that, but let's start with how it's possible to go from her wanting to get away from you to what we just saw outside. I wasn't sure she was ever going to let you go."

Deacon probably couldn't see that while Kaia was struggling to tear herself away from me, I was battling just the same to let her go.

Playing it cool, I replied, "What can I say? I'm irresistible."

"Yeah, okay," Vaughn responded. "Now, what's the real truth?"

I didn't actually think they'd believe me, but it was worth a shot. "It's actually pretty simple," I started. "She had planned to make Monday night her last night there. I wasn't the least bit interested in entertaining that idea, so I did what I had to do to convince her to stay."

My brothers stared at me in silence for several moments before Vaughn asked, "And that worked?"

I grinned at them. "Like I said… I'm irresistible."

Now it was his turn to roll his eyes.

"Can we talk about how before she succumbed to your charm, she was ready to move back into an apartment where she'd already been attacked three times?" Deacon asked. "Is she not worried about that guy approaching her again?"

"She is, but she was having a hard time trying to resist

me," I explained. "So, she thought it would be better to put some distance between us."

"Remi, I'm being serious," Deacon asserted.

"So am I," I assured him. "I didn't know that initially, and she had tried to convince me that it was just time for her to go since the TRO was in place. But I ended up finding out later that she's not exactly confident about her ex's ability to refrain from approaching her again."

"So, she's still staying with you now, right?" Vaughn asked.

"Yep."

"And you two are clearly together now, correct?" Deacon pressed.

"Yep."

There was a brief pause before Vaughn said, "Congratulations, Remi. I hope it works out for the two of you."

"Thanks, Vaughn."

My eyes shifted to Deacon, who let out a laugh. "I knew it was never going to remain professional," he declared.

Vaughn and I both laughed.

A moment later, Deacon said, "I really am happy for you, Remi. Maybe this is weird, but I want to say I'm even happier for her. Because at least now she's with someone who's going to treat her the way she deserves to be treated."

"Yeah," Vaughn agreed. "It honestly blows my mind how resilient she seems. I mean, I haven't really had much of an opportunity to talk to her. Still, knowing what we know now about why her former relationship ended, I have to say I'm impressed by her ability to push forward with such determination."

"It's because she's had a good teacher," I said.

"Still singing your own praises," Deacon muttered. "Man, can't you even give the girl credit for her own capability?"

"I'm not talking about me," I told him. "I'm talking about her sister."

"Her sister?" Vaughn repeated.

Nodding, I explained, "Her sister, Parker, showed her what she was worth. If Kaia doesn't stand up and fight for herself, it makes everything Parker did pointless."

Confusion washed over both of their faces, but it was Deacon who asked, "What did her sister do?"

"Kaia and Parker were raised by an abusive father," I started and instantly noticed their bodies lock. "Any time their father got angry, Parker put herself in harm's way to protect Kaia. Now that Kaia is here on her own and found herself in the line of fire, she did what she had to do to protect herself."

"Fuck," Deacon clipped. "Are you telling us that her father beat her and her sister?"

"It happened to her three times, but that's because Parker stepped up and sacrificed herself to keep her baby sister safe. My guess is Kaia witnessed it more than she experienced it."

Vaughn and Deacon both shook their heads in disgust. I didn't want this conversation to end on such a bitter note, so I decided to give them something else.

"Hey, listen, I'm going to need to rework a few things in the schedule for early next week," I told them.

"Why? What's going on?"

"Kaia wants to tell her sister what's been happening in her life over the last few weeks, but she doesn't want to do it over the phone," I answered. "We're going to catch a flight out on Sunday morning, and we will be back late Wednesday night. I should be back in to work on Thursday morning."

"That's cool. Do whatever you've got to do to help her," Vaughn urged. "Where are you headed?"

"Rising Sun."

"What?"

"Parker still lives in the place she and Kaia grew up. Rising Sun, Wyoming."

"You're shitting me!" Deacon exclaimed.

I shook my head. "Nope."

"Are you going to visit Monroe and introduce them?" Vaughn asked.

"That was my plan."

"That's unbelievable," Deacon declared. "What are the chances?"

"Crazy, right?" I said. "I don't know, I'm not one of those people who believe in signs or anything like that, but I feel like this is a big deal."

Vaughn and Deacon stood there in silence for a bit, digesting the news. I couldn't say I blamed them. It came as just as much of a surprise to me—a good surprise, but a surprise nonetheless.

"Anyway, if you have anything you want to send out for the kids, just get it to me before Sunday," I said.

"Sounds good."

"Alright, we need to get to work," I suggested.

And with that, we got back to work. Then, and because she had said she was going to miss me, I found a way to leave work a little bit earlier than usual to surprise Kaia before she had to go to work.

Luckily for me, I timed it just right so that we had some time to play before she needed to go.

Kaia

"Hey, Kaia!"

I continued my trek to the bar, where Bianca and Skylar were gathered together.

"Hey," I greeted them. "How's it going?"

"Good," Bianca answered. "We're just doing the usual."

"The usual?" I asked.

"Complaining about our husbands," Skylar clarified. "What else?"

I let out a laugh. "Oh no. What did they do now?" I wondered.

Shaking her head, Skylar said, "Nothing specific."

"And that's precisely the problem," Bianca chimed in. "They've done nothing. Do you know how infuriating it is to ask your husband like a million times to do that one simple thing around the house, and months later, he still hasn't done it?"

"I can't imagine it would make me happy," I said.

Bianca was a bit fired up and went on, "I've been working on some landscaping at our house and started telling Ken months ago about my plan. He listened or pretended to anyway. And then, when I had finally got to the point that I needed his help with pulling out a bunch of the shrubs that have been there since we moved in, he balked at the job. Like, come on. I told you about this months ago. I wasn't going outside just so I could work on my tan every day."

I wanted to laugh again but decided against it. Bianca

was clearly riled up. Instead of responding to that, I looked at Skylar and asked, "How's Cole?"

"Don't get me started," she muttered. "How are you doing? I feel like we haven't seen each other in ages."

"I know. All things considered, I'm doing really well," I told her.

"I still can't believe what Nolan did," Bianca declared. "I mean, Ken gets pissed at me for giving him shit about housework and stuff, but he'd never do anything like that to me. I'm so angry for you, Kaia."

"Thanks, B."

As it turned out, when Deacon made the call to Matt, the owner of Club Infinity, and explained the situation, the news made its way to Bianca. I wasn't necessarily upset about her knowing so much as I would have preferred being the one to share it. But because this was an unpredictable situation and nobody knew how Nolan would react, Matt had to share the news with the necessary staff members.

The first day I came into work after Bianca learned the truth, she called me into her office, where she and Skylar were waiting with concerned looks and listening ears. I shared the truth with them, and of course, they were thrilled to hear all about how I'd defended myself against Nolan in the parking lot outside my apartment complex.

"So, listen, we know you've got to get over there and get yourself ready," Skylar said as she jerked her head toward the DJ booth. "But before you go, we wanted to see if you were free to get together for brunch on Sunday or lunch on Monday."

"I'm sorry. I wish I could," I lamented. "I'm actually making a quick trip out to visit my sister. I want to fill her in on what's been happening here while I gobble up some time with my niece. But I'm down for getting together the following Sunday if that works."

"That works for me," Bianca said. "I'm sure my shrubs still won't be gone by then, so I'll have nothing to do."

Through her laughter, Skylar announced, "Next Sunday works for me, too."

"Cool. We'll talk specifics next week," I reasoned.

"Okay. Kick some ass tonight," Skylar urged.

"She's DJ Banks," Bianca declared. "Of course, she's going to kick ass."

I shook my head as I smiled and walked away. Only a few minutes after I'd made it over to my booth, there was a knock at the door.

I turned around and saw Juan standing there. "Hey, Juan. How's it going? Are you on with me tonight?"

"You know it," he returned. "I just thought I'd come up here and find out what kind of trouble you got yourself into since the last time I saw you."

"It hasn't even been a full week," I pointed out. "What kind of trouble do you think I could possibly get into in a matter of a few days?"

"With you, Banks, it's anyone's guess," he stated.

I grinned at him. He didn't return the grin, but there was a lip twitch.

That's when I said, "Well, I'll have you know that I've been a very good girl and haven't started any fights or beat anyone up. But that's probably mostly because I've been too busy with my new boyfriend."

"Boyfriend?" Juan repeated. "Banks, you're killing me here."

I lifted my hands out to the side and shrugged my

shoulders. "He was too hot to resist, Juan. What do you want from me?"

"Where did you meet this guy? Do I need to open a private investigation firm so I can look into this guy before things get too serious?" he questioned me.

My brows pulled together. Did the man have no faith at all in me?

"If you did that, who would guard my booth?" I teased.

"Maybe nobody would need to if I did that," he shot back.

I harrumphed. "Relax, big guy. You don't need to worry about starting a new career just because of me," I assured him. "My new boyfriend would check out okay anyway."

Juan narrowed his eyes on me. "How can you be so sure?"

"Because it's Remi."

"Really?" he asked.

I nodded. "Yep. I told the man I was going to move back home, and he convinced me to stay."

Juan put his hand up. "I don't need the details, Banks," he insisted. "But I'm glad for you. Remi's a good dude, and I have no concerns about your safety with him."

"He's hot, too," I said, knowing I was going to make him crazy.

"I don't know. That's not my area of expertise," he replied.

"And he's so good with—"

"Stop!" Juan ordered. "I don't want to know. Just do your thing, and be happy."

I laughed before I murmured, "Thanks for being such a good friend, Juan. It means a lot to know I have people I can count on."

"You know I've always got your back, Banks," he said. He

paused a moment before he continued, "I'll be outside. Make it a good night tonight."

And that was precisely what I did.

In fact, it was better than good. It was phenomenal.

What made it even better was that Remi had left work early because he wanted to see me before I had to go. He ended up dropping me off at work on his way back to Archer Tactical. And I knew that once my night was over, he'd be waiting outside to pick me up.

But that wasn't what happened. Instead, once the night had ended and I walked out of my booth, I found that Remi didn't wait outside for me. He'd come in to wait for me at the bottom of the stairs. He'd been talking to Juan, but once he heard the door open and looked up at me, Juan no longer existed.

I loved the way he looked at me.

Like I was some precious jewel he was given the duty to protect.

I descended the stairs, said goodbye to Juan, and introduced Skylar to Remi before he led me out of the club and to his car.

That's when I realized Juan was wrong. Remi wasn't just a good dude. He cared about me in a way no man had ever done before him. He was, without a doubt, perfect for me. And that... well, it had me struggling not to fall hard and fast for him.

CHAPTER 16

Kaia

MY MOANS FILLED THE ROOM AS I GREW MORE AND
more excited about what I was doing.

It was late Sunday morning, and Remi and I had
arrived in Wyoming about an hour ago. After we left Rising
Sun International Airport, Remi rented a car and drove us to
a hotel so we could drop off our things and get settled before
we took off to go see my sister, Nash, and Wren.

But no sooner did we get into the hotel room when I
looked over at Remi and felt something come over me.

I didn't know what it was. I couldn't explain it. The emotions hit me so hard, and all I could do was react to what I felt.

While my sister was expecting me today, I'd given her a
fake time for my arrival. That meant I'd have plenty of time to
accomplish this and get to her place before she even thought
about sending Nash out to pick me up while she stayed home
with Wren.

And it was a good thing I thought ahead. Of course, my

reason for giving her that fake time was because I wanted to surprise her.

But her surprise was just going to have to wait a little bit longer because we were going to be arriving at my sister's place a little later than I had anticipated.

I was enjoying this too much, and I had no intention of stopping.

Remi had brought our bags in and set them down, and the only thing I wanted to do was get my mouth on him. So, before he could start walking back toward where I was standing closer to the door, I moved to him.

When I came to a stop in front of him and shot him a devious smile, he asked, "What's going on?"

"Nothing," I lied, urging him to sit down on the bed.

He didn't resist.

Then, I got to work.

I lifted his shirt up over his head and tossed it aside. With his bare chest on display, my fingertips traced delicately over his smooth skin before they moved south and landed on the fly of his jeans.

Feeling such need pulsing through me, I worked quickly to unbutton and unzip his jeans to free him. I pulled out his cock and wasted not one second getting him in my mouth.

He tasted incredible.

Now, I'd been here a while, and I was totally in the zone. I loved what I was doing to him. Hearing the groans coming from deep at the back of his throat and feeling his grip in my hair tighten, I couldn't help but feel myself grow more excited.

I licked. I sucked. I stroked.

I worked the tip, bringing my tongue out to swirl and

tease. I took him in deep, feeling him hit the back of my throat and never wanting to pull myself back.

All I wanted to do was drive him wild.

And I was. I knew I was.

But I wondered if I could get more pleasure from what I was doing to him than he was actually getting from it.

If nothing else, I knew I was getting lost in it far more than he was. Though, I only realized that when I had him there in my mouth, and suddenly, he was gone.

Remi had put his hands under my armpits and hauled me up his body as he fell to his back in the bed.

Wrapping his arms around me, he asked, "Are you purposely ignoring me?"

My brows pulled together in my confusion, but I didn't get a chance to ask him what he meant because the next thing I knew, Remi flipped me to my back, yanked my shorts and panties down my legs, and pushed my legs open so he could feast on me.

And boy did he feast.

Since we'd officially gotten together, Remi had gone down on me several times. I was convinced it got better each and every time.

Almost instantly, he had me panting. "Remi, babe."

He groaned against me, continuing his delicious torture on my sensitive clit.

Both of my hands drove into his hair, settled at the back of his head, and held him there. My hips moved against him, seeking more friction. More Remi.

He pressed my legs open wider and gripped my thighs tighter.

"I need more," I begged. "Please."

Remi didn't stop. He continued to lick and suck and taste and tease. His relentless assault on me was building me up quickly, and I had a feeling he knew it.

"Don't stop," I pleaded. "Oh, God, I'm going to come."

Remi growled and applied more pressure as one of his hands flew up to my breast and squeezed.

Seconds later, it happened.

Pleasure shot through me, and my legs trembled on either side of his head. Remi worked me through my orgasm, slowing the movements of his tongue until he eventually stopped.

I thought I'd get a break, but I barely had half a minute to come down from the high when Remi was flipping me over to my belly, gripping my hips in his hands, and lifting me up onto my knees.

Then, he was driving inside me.

"Fuck, baby, you're so beautiful. You feel beautiful," he professed. His voice was a mix of adoration and huskiness.

I tipped my ass higher, curled my fingers into the blanket, and held on. Twisting my neck, I looked back at him and our eyes locked.

"Harder," I demanded, rearing back on him.

His fingers gripped me firmly, and he gave it to me harder.

Eventually, one of his hands moved from my hip to come around and find my clit. He played. He used his hands to play while he continued to stroke his cock in and out of me.

A moment later, Remi's free arm came across my chest and lifted me up so my back was to his front. There, he kept one hand between my legs while the other squeezed, touched, teased, and played with my breasts. Not once throughout it did his hips stop surging forward.

"Remi," I called out my warning.

"Are you going to come for me, Kaia?"

"Yes," I whimpered loudly. "Yes. Please don't stop. You feel so good."

"You like it?"

"I love it. I love your cock," I moaned.

Remi held me firmly against him, thrust his hips forward powering himself deep inside me, and never stopped until not only I cried out, shaking and trembling from the force of it all, but he did, too.

It was magnificent.

Remi and I collapsed on the bed and fought to regain control of our breathing. After some time, he moved to the bathroom to dispose of the condom.

I'd just barely gotten my lungs functioning correctly again when he returned and declared, "I don't know what brought that on, but I'd love to know what it was so I can make sure to do it again."

I let out a laugh and shared, "You were there."

Remi flopped down on the bed next to me. We were both on our backs, and he looked over at me.

"I was there?" he asked.

"No. I… I don't know how to explain it," I stammered. "I just… something about seeing you there at that moment did something inside me. And all I could think about was making you feel as good as you've made me feel these last couple of weeks. That's all."

"Good to know," he replied.

I took in a deep breath, trying to make sure I'd gotten my breathing back to normal again. Then I sighed, "Parker is going to lose her mind."

"Because you insisted on keeping me a secret?" he guessed.

I shook my head. "Nope. Well, I mean, I'm sure she's going to freak out about that, but that's not what I was referring to."

"So, what is it?" he asked.

"I'm staying in a hotel instead of staying with them," I declared.

"Yeah, but once she knows that I'm with you, I'm sure she'll be fine with it," he reasoned.

I shook my head. "No. She'd rather the two of us stay there with her, Nash, and Wren."

"Sweetheart, that can't happen," he deadpanned.

"I realize we're here now, but why do you seem so serious about it?" I asked. "I mean, we could always just stay here tonight and check out in the morning if she pushes us to stay with her."

"We're not staying with them," he insisted.

His tone caught me by surprise.

"Is everything okay?" I asked.

"Kaia, baby, they have a new baby," he told me as though I didn't already know.

"What does that have to do with anything?"

His eyes widened in surprise and disbelief. "Are you kidding me?"

I shook my head and gave him a look of confusion. He wasn't making a damn bit of sense.

"Okay, I'm going to break this down for you," he started. "We're here for a few days without either one of us needing to go to work. We've got all this time together. And I know we'll be spending the days with either your sister and her family or my sister and her family. But at night, you're mine, and I want to enjoy you."

"You could still do that. I'm sure Parker understands that we're two consenting adults," I assured him.

"I'm sure she does, but do you want her to hear you?"

"What?" I gasped.

"Kaia, you are not quiet during sex, and you don't hold yourself back from saying what you're feeling," he shared. My body tensed. Remi noticed and placed his hand on my thigh. After giving it a squeeze, he insisted, "Don't get weird on me now. I love it. But I'm thinking you probably don't want to wake your niece up because you're begging me to fuck you."

"I don't beg," I argued.

"Baby, you do," he asserted. "Hell, you love it so much, you never even heard me speaking when you had my cock in your mouth."

"What are you talking about? You didn't say anything," I contended.

He laughed. "Yes, I did. And you know what? I don't give a shit that you didn't hear me. You were that into it, loving what you were doing and seriously turned on by it. And don't try to say that you weren't because by the time I put my mouth between your legs, you were already soaked."

I bit my lip. *Was it too much?*

Remi rolled to his side, propped his head up in his hand, and brought his free hand to the side of my face. After his thumb freed my lip from the confines of my teeth, his voice got soft, and he said, "Don't you dare even think about being anybody other than who you are when we're together like this. Hearing you like that, whether you're begging for me to fuck you harder or you're moaning because you love what I'm giving you, is a huge turn-on. And you make me come hard, Kaia. If you take that away from me, I'm going to be pissed."

The tension left my body, and I rolled onto my side. Burying my face in his chest, I felt nothing but an overwhelming sense of relief.

His hand stroked gently up and down my naked back as he kissed my head through my hair.

After a bit, he asked, "Are you okay?"

"Yeah," I answered. "I think you're right. We should stay here. I don't want to traumatize my niece, my sister, or my brother-in-law."

Remi chuckled. "Good idea. And just so you know, my sister is going to be the same exact way as yours. She'll want us to stay with them. I don't care what she says; the answer is no. I definitely don't need my sister or any of my nieces or nephews hearing what I'm doing to you."

"I'm so lucky you think about things like this," I said.

"You mean having sex with you?" he asked. "I think about that more frequently than is probably reasonable. And you know what? I don't care."

I tipped my head back and looked up at him. He smiled down at me. I lifted up and kissed him. When I pulled back, I said, "I should probably get cleaned up so we can get out of here."

His hand, which had drifted down to my ass, gave me a squeeze. "Okay. Go get yourself ready, so we can pull off your surprise. If we stay in this bed any longer with you being naked, I'm going to need to have some fun with you again."

"No!" I cried as I sat up. "We have to leave. Get some clothes on before you distract me again."

"Having all my clothes on before didn't seem to thwart your mission," he reminded me.

I growled. Maybe he was telling the truth. That didn't

mean he needed to point out how weak I was when it came to him. It just wasn't nice.

Before I did something I would regret, only because it would ruin the surprise I had planned for my sister, I got up and grabbed some clothes and made my way into the bathroom to get myself cleaned up and ready.

Ten minutes later, Remi and I had left the hotel and were on our way to see Parker and her family.

I couldn't wait to get there and see her reaction.

Of course, all the shock she'd feel would quickly fade away to be replaced by utter joy and happiness at seeing me. But that, too, would vanish when she met Remi. I'd have to tell her the story of how we met, why I went to Archer Tactical to begin with, and I'd devastate her.

I didn't know how I was going to do it, but I knew I needed to.

So, just as I always seemed to do when I needed it, I mustered up some courage, determination, and confidence and prepared myself for what was to come.

Before I knew it, Remi and I had arrived at Parker and Nash's home. And just as I suspected, when she opened the door and saw me, there was nothing but shock written all over her face.

"Kaia?" she gasped.

"Surprise," I returned.

She stared at me for several long moments before her eyes darted to my side at Remi and back again. Then a big smile formed on her face, and she pulled me into a hug.

"Oh, I missed you so much," she declared.

I hugged her back and replied, "I missed you, too."

When we separated, she looked at Remi again. That's when I said, "Parker, this is Remi. Remi, this is Parker."

Remi held his hand out to her and said, "It's so nice to finally meet you."

"Finally?" she countered.

Uh oh.

Remi indicated he'd known about her, but she obviously hadn't once heard me mention his name.

Damn it.

I had a feeling Parker was going to be hurt. When she returned her gaze to me, I no longer had any doubt about it. Parker had likely just figured out that Remi was my new guy, and I'd said nothing to her.

"What's going on?" she rasped.

I felt nothing but defeat wash over me. Despite it, I insisted, "Parker, we need to talk."

CHAPTER 17

Kaia

THERE WAS NO MISTAKING THE TENSION IN THE AIR as Remi and I followed behind my sister into the home she shared with Nash.

I hated it.

This was not how I intended to have this go. Part of me believed that I'd done the right thing in waiting to tell Parker until I could do it face-to-face, but the other part of me felt nervous. We never really fought with one another, so this was new territory for me.

Parker was my sister; I knew she'd never stay mad forever. But I hated to think I'd done anything to make her lose her faith and trust in me.

Only time would tell if this feeling would go away. I was sure it wouldn't happen until she at least heard what I had to say.

Once we entered the family room, I looked around for Wren, but she wasn't in her bassinet or her swing.

"Where's Wren?" I asked.

"Nash just took her upstairs to put her down for a nap," Parker answered. "We're trying to transition her to her crib for naptime."

Just then, we heard the footsteps descending the stairs. At the pace they were moving, I had to assume Nash got my niece down for her nap and no longer had her in his arms.

Sure enough, Nash entered the room a moment later, carrying the baby monitor in his hand. Surprise washed over him as his eyes moved back and forth between Remi and me. Ultimately, they settled on mine as he moved toward me, gave me a hug, and said, "You're here. I thought I was coming to pick you up."

"I wanted to surprise you two," I replied.

As he pulled back, he said, "Well, you certainly accomplished that. It's good to see you again. How was your flight?"

Smiling, I returned, "You too. And the flight was okay." When Nash's eyes went to Remi's again, I shook my head of the thoughts I still had lingering about my sister and lamented, "I'm sorry. Nash, this is Remi. Remi, this is Nash."

For the first time since Nash had entered the room, I looked at Remi. A strange look had washed over his face. I couldn't read it, and it was making me feel a little uneasy to see because, if nothing else, I knew he was assessing Nash. Something about it just felt off.

And when I took a moment to think about Remi and the guy he was, I really started to worry. Because if there was one thing I thought Remi could do exceptionally well, it was reading people. With the look he was shooting in Nash's direction, considering it wasn't one I'd ever seen, I had to wonder if he was getting a bad vibe from him.

Eventually, and luckily, whatever it was, Remi ignored it and extended his hand to Nash. They shook hands before Nash urged, "Have a seat."

Remi and I sat down as Nash moved back toward Parker. She settled herself on the opposite side of the L-shaped couch from us, and the worried look still hadn't left her face. Of course, Nash proved he could be observant, too. At least, he was when it came to Parker.

"What's going on?" he asked her, not missing the look on her face. "Are you okay?"

"I don't know," she rasped.

Nash lifted his gaze toward us.

That's when I said, "I have some news to share, and I didn't want to do it over the phone."

Understanding dawned in Nash's expression as I felt Remi's hand reach over to mine. Parker's eyes dropped to our connection, and I could see her mind working.

"Oh my God," she gasped. "Are you pregnant?"

"What? No!" I exclaimed. "Where would you come up with an idea like that?"

"I'm sorry," she lamented. "It's just that… this is strange. If that's not it, what else could there possibly be that you wouldn't want to tell me over the phone?"

I looked over at Remi; he squeezed my hand and offered an encouraging smile. Returning my attention to my sister, I reminded her, "Remember how I told you things had ended between Nolan and me?"

"Yeah."

"Well, there's a reason for that," I announced. "And I think you should know what it is."

Nash must have read something in the situation

because his expression turned serious as he wrapped an arm around Parker's back and settled his hand on her opposite shoulder.

"He was beating me," I blurted.

Shit.

I hadn't meant for it to come out like that.

In an instant, Parker's hand flew up to cover her mouth as tears filled her eyes. "What?" she mumbled behind her hand. "What do you mean? How long? Are you okay?"

God.

My sister.

I loved her more than I could ever put into words.

I gave her a moment to collect herself and noticed that even Nash was not happy. But where Parker was emotional and sad, Nash was angry.

"I'm sorry to say this, considering you obviously liked the guy at some point, but I knew there was a reason I never liked him much at all," Nash declared.

Parker's head snapped in his direction. "What? You didn't like him? Why didn't you say anything?" she questioned him.

"What should I have said? Kaia is your sister. She was happy. You were happy. I wasn't in their relationship, so I could have been wrong about my feeling," he reasoned.

"You obviously weren't," Parker noted.

Not wanting my problems to cause turmoil for them, I interrupted, "It wasn't all bad from the start. And after the first time it happened, it was over for me. Of course, that didn't stop him from thinking that I was going to stay with him anyway. But I'm trying to tell you that I didn't stick around for it. I didn't endure months and months of abuse.

There were three separate incidences. The first time it happened was just a couple days after I got back from visiting you after Wren was born. In that incident and one other, he got the best of me. In the last, I took him down."

Nash's brows shot up in surprise, and Parker's body went solid. "What?" she asked.

Remi chimed in at that point and proudly stated, "She elbowed him in the face before she kicked him in the balls."

Nash made a hissing sound as though hearing the words was an assault to his own manhood while Parker's mouth simply dropped open.

I looked to my side and saw Remi sitting there with a massive smile on his face. He was still so proud of me.

Then, for the first time ever, he winked at me. If this hadn't been such a tense situation, I might have jumped on him right then and there. Who knew a wink could make me feel so much?

Even though Remi gave me a momentary high, I had to quickly come back down to reality.

And that happened when Parker lamented, "I'm sorry, but I feel like I'm missing a lot here."

"Parker—" I started before she cut me off.

Her gaze was pinned on Remi. "Who exactly are you?"

"Remington Archer," he answered. "And I'm dating your sister."

Remington.

He was being official.

How did I not know that Remi was a nickname?

I had about a million things I wanted to discuss with him at that point, but I couldn't because Parker looked right at him and said, "Dating?"

Remi nodded. "Yes."

There was a moment of silence before Parker stated, "I hope you'll take no offense to this, but it sounds to me like my sister just recently went through a breakup. I'm not sure dating is a smart idea right now."

"Parker?" I called.

"What?" she asked.

"Please don't do this," I begged.

Her eyes filled with tears. "Somebody hurt you," she croaked. "Somebody hurt you, and I wasn't there to protect you. And now you're moving on, and I feel like it's really fast. I don't want you to get hurt again."

"I can't help what I feel," I rasped.

"I would never lay a hand on her," Remi chimed in. "Never would I raise my hands to her. Parker, I'm giving you my word; you don't have to worry."

"She's my sister. I'll always worry."

Nodding, Remi insisted, "I know. I get that."

"I'm sorry," she apologized. "Like I said, I don't want you to take offense to this. I'm sure you're a nice guy, but I don't know you, and my only concern is my sister."

"But Kaia isn't your only concern," he pointed out, though his voice was gentle.

"Excuse me?"

"You have a husband and a new daughter, who I know is your top priority. I know that's the case because even though I don't know you very well yet, I know who you were to Kaia growing up, and I'm sure you already have those same protective instincts with your daughter," Remi remarked. He gave Parker a moment to digest that information before he continued, "There is nobody in this world who can ever question how much you love your sister. What you did for her, what you endured so she wouldn't have to, is beyond courageous and filled with love. All I'm saying is that you'll always have that. You can look back if you need to and know that you did what you needed to do for her. And because you did it, she grew up to be the resilient, strong woman that she is today. She's now a woman who is tough enough to fight back and protect herself while still finding a way to keep her heart open to finding love. You gave that to her. Let me give her the rest."

My heart.

This man.

Right there, at that moment, I fell so deep in love with him.

He wanted to give me the rest.

Even if I didn't know all that the rest entailed, I knew I wanted it.

I could just barely see the tears streaming down Parker's face since my eyes had filled with tears of their own.

When Parker didn't respond, Remi encouraged gently, "You can let her go, Parker. I promise you, she's in good hands."

I swiped at the tears that had trickled down my cheeks and shared, "He's good to me. He treats me with respect, he looks out for me, and he's the only reason I was able to defend myself the last time Nolan tried to attack me."

"What does that mean?" Nash asked. "Why was he the reason you could defend yourself?"

His tone was genuinely curious, not accusatory. I so appreciated his willingness to stay levelheaded when Parker and I were both so emotional. In fact, I appreciated that both Nash and Remi were staying calm.

"Remi is part owner of a company called Archer Tactical," I answered. "While there's a wide range of services and training they offer, he's been teaching me self-defense. I was given the name of his company by the guy in charge of security at Club Infinity, Juan."

A look of surprise and maybe a bit of respect washed over Nash. My eyes slid to Parker's. "Remi and his team of men are responsible for the training that Juan and many members of his team have received. And if the fact that Remi's part of a team that's responsible for teaching civilians how to protect themselves and their communities isn't enough proof of who this man is, then maybe the fact that they do training drills with SWAT and other law enforcement officials will be. Remi is one of the good guys, Parker. I really need you to believe that."

"Will you tell me everything that happened?" Parker asked after she'd taken some time to consider what I'd just shared.

"I'll tell you everything you want to know," I replied.

"I want to know all of it," she insisted.

So, I told her everything. I started at the beginning, which was when I returned from my trip to Rising Sun when Wren was born. It ended with me showing up on her doorstep today with Remi by my side. Throughout it all, neither Parker nor Nash interrupted. And I didn't leave out any details of what I'd been through. Some of it was harder to share than others, but I did my best to stay strong while I shared. Not only did I know that it'd only make Parker more upset than she already was to see me upset, but I knew it would help her more to see me strong and pushing through.

When I finished, which took some time, I noticed Parker was looking at me with an expression similar to the one Remi had when he announced I'd kicked Nolan in the balls. It was one filled with pride.

"I'm so proud of you, Kaia," she said when I'd ended my story.

"Thank you," I returned. "And Remi was right, you know?"

"About what?"

"You're the reason I am who I am today, Parker," I declared, doing my best to speak through the tightening in my throat. "I wouldn't be half the woman I am if I didn't have you."

Parker stood from the couch, moved toward me as I did the same, and threw her arms around me when she made it to me. I hugged her back, squeezing tight.

"I love you, Kaia," she whispered.

"I love you, too."

We held each other for a bit before eventually separating. When we did, Parker looked down at Remi and said, "I'm letting her go and trusting you to take care of her. Don't make me regret it."

Remi stood and promised, "You have nothing to worry about."

She nodded slowly. "I hope that's true."

"I'm the oldest of four kids," Remi shared. "Two younger brothers and a younger sister. I feel the same about them that you do about Kaia. So, believe me when I say I understand where you're coming from."

"Remi's taking me to meet his sister later today," I interjected.

I watched as confusion littered my sister's face. "I thought you were staying here until Wednesday," she said.

I let out a laugh. "We are. Believe it or not, Remi's sister lives here in Rising Sun."

Confusion turned to surprise. "Really?" Parker asked.

"I had the same reaction when I found out," I told her. "She's married with four kids."

"Wow," Parker marveled.

That's when Remi jumped in and said, "I'm going to take Kaia over to meet my sister, my brother-in-law, and the kids today. And if you guys are up to it, I'll talk to Monroe and Stone about possibly having all of us get together before Kaia and I head back to Poppy Valley."

"Stone?" Nash said. "Stone is your brother-in-law?"

"Yeah," Remi answered. "Is that how I know you? I've been trying to figure out this whole time where I know you from."

Well, that explained the strange look that had washed over Remi when he first met Nash earlier. He hadn't been sizing Nash up or regarding him in a way that meant he didn't like it. He simply recognized him and couldn't place him.

Nash grinned. "I'm the chassis tuner at LT Motorsports," Nash shared. "We must have met at the shop or one of Stone's events."

"I thought I was going crazy," Remi declared.

"I don't understand," I said. "I thought you said Stone was a snowboarder."

"He is," Remi insisted. "But during the off-season, he

192

races. Or, he used to anyway. Now he does stuff like that for fun only occasionally because he's too busy raising four kids with my sister."

A small cry rang through the air. As though she knew there was talk of kids in the air and she wasn't the center of the conversation, my niece woke up from her nap.

"Oh, that's my favorite girl," I squealed.

"I'll go get her," Nash announced, already making his way to the stairs.

"I'll get everybody drinks," Parker stated as she turned and walked off to the kitchen.

Once we were alone, Remi turned me in his arms and said, "Are you okay?"

I smiled at him and nodded. "Yeah, I am now. I'm sorry about how Parker reacted. She's just protective of me."

"Don't worry about that," he insisted. "I'm glad you have her."

"Did you mean all that stuff you said?" I asked.

"Well, I don't know which stuff you're specifically referring to, but there wasn't anything I lied about this afternoon either," he assured me. "So yes, I meant all that stuff."

I lifted my hand to his hair and ran my fingers through it. "Thank you for being here with me today," I said softly.

"You're welcome, sweetheart," he replied before he kissed my cheek.

A few minutes later, Nash returned with Wren. I didn't wait for him to bring her to me. I shot up off the couch, ran over to him, and scooped her out of his arms.

Walking back toward Remi, I declared, "Here she is... the most beautiful baby in the world."

"She's adorable," Remi agreed.

And if I wasn't convinced I'd already fallen in love with him when he told my sister he wanted to give me the rest, it would have happened when, after he'd given me some time to cuddle her, he asked if he could have a turn to hold her.

Seeing him holding Wren like she was the most precious thing in the world was all I needed for me to know that he was the one for me. He accepted me the way I was, reassured my sister and eased her fears, and he liked babies.

There was no doubt about it.

I was in love with Remington Archer.

CHAPTER 18

Remi

"SO SHE REALLY KICKED HIM IN THE BALLS?"

I let out a laugh as I looked away from where Kaia was sitting to my right. Nash was standing beside me, and when he felt my attention on him, he shifted his gaze in my direction.

Nodding, I confirmed, "Yep. Though I never saw it happen, I heard about it within minutes afterward. You should have seen how jazzed up Kaia was about it."

Nash grinned. "Good for her."

It was now Tuesday afternoon, and Kaia and I had returned to my sister's house for another visit. This time, Parker, Nash, and Wren were here with us.

When Kaia and I came alone on Sunday, I was relieved to see she hit it off with my sister right away. Then again, Monroe had always been a big ball of love, so I never really doubted it to begin with anyway. Once Monroe found out what Kaia did for a living, it just took things to the next level. Not only did Kaia and Monroe get along, but Kaia was also high up on the kids' lists because she arrived with me and carried in a few gifts. In the eyes of my nieces and nephews, even if they weren't wrapped, presents made you a cool person.

Later that evening, I shared the news with Stone and Monroe that Kaia's sister lived close. As soon as they knew, they insisted on having them over before we returned to California. Of course, they couldn't get over what a small world it really was when they learned that Kaia's sister was married to Nash, who Stone had known for years from his off-season racing.

So, now we were here like one big happy family.

Stone was in the swimming pool with Archer, Harper, and Phoenix while Kaia, Parker, and Monroe were sitting under the shade of the covered deck with Wren and Tessa. Nash and I were standing off to the side with a view of everyone, and we were far enough away that nobody would hear the specifics of our conversation.

Though the conversation had started out lighthearted, I had a feeling that was soon going to change. Maybe it was merely my gut instinct, or perhaps it was the fact that I believed Nash was a lot like me when it came to protecting and caring for the woman in his life. Still, I just knew he had things he wanted to discuss with me that he could not discuss at any point over the last two days when Kaia and Parker were present the entire time.

"Yeah, I'm really proud of her," I replied. "She learned quickly and managed to put a fair amount of what she was taught into action. I just wish she would have told me sooner about the whole situation."

"She's a tough cookie," Nash noted.

I looked back in her direction and chuckled. "You have no idea," I said. "She was so shocked by what she'd done. It wasn't regret, though. It was merely surprise that she was capable of taking him down."

"As happy as I am to know that she's learning all the skills necessary to defend herself, do you think she's going to need to use them again? In your professional opinion, what would you say about the possibility of this guy following the rules of the restraining order and staying away from her?" Nash asked.

And there it was.

I knew he had something far more serious he wanted to discuss. Sadly, I didn't have any answers for him.

"I wish I could tell you what you want to hear," I admitted. "But I honestly don't know."

"So, there's no telling if he's gone for good and we have nothing left to worry about? I'm still going to have to prepare myself for the genuine possibility that a call is going to come from California that's going to send my wife reeling worse than it did the day you and Kaia arrived?"

I sighed. "Unfortunately, that's the sad truth," I told him. "I'd love nothing more than to be able to stand here and tell you that it's all over and there's nothing to worry about, but I'd be lying. I don't know this guy; I've never met him. But given the fact that you have and you didn't get a good vibe from the start and are now asking me these questions, I get the feeling you already know the answer."

"Fuck," he hissed. "I was afraid you'd say something like that."

"Listen, Nash, you and I can stand here and think that any logical person who had a restraining order against them would not do anything to risk facing criminal charges and jail time for violating that order," I began. "But the reality is that most people who have restraining orders against them aren't exactly using good judgment all the time. So, no matter how much I want to believe that Kaia seeing to it means that this asshole would face charges is enough to convince him to stay away, I just don't know if that's the case."

"What are you going to do about it?" he asked.

"Exactly what I've been training my whole life to do," I answered. "I'm going to see to it that she stays safe. She's staying with me right now, and this guy would be an idiot if he found out she was there and decided to try his luck at my place."

"What if she wants to go home?" Nash wondered.

It was a reasonable question. Things between Kaia and I were still new. And even though I had no doubt about who she was and what she meant to me, I realized she was dealing with a lot. It would have been wrong for me to not understand that she might need her own space.

"I'm going to do what I can to keep her with me at my place, where I'm certain he doesn't know she is just yet," I started as I returned my gaze to Nash. "But if she decides she wants to go back home to her place, I'll give her what she needs. I'll just do it knowing I'm going to give her that while doing whatever I've got to do to keep her safe."

A look of approval washed over him. I think he realized, if nothing else, I wasn't a liar. I couldn't make promises about what somebody else would do. All I could do was give my word that I'd do whatever was necessary to protect Kaia.

He took in a deep breath and blew it out as he returned his attention to where the women were sitting.

"I mean absolutely no offense to your sister, but those two sisters are something else," he declared.

"None taken because I fully understand what you're getting at," I assured him. "I only know what I know about Parker from Kaia and from what I've seen over the last couple of days. Amazingly, they've gone through all that they have and come out the other side not just alive but with that much love to give."

"They're stronger than I think they even realize," Nash stated.

"I completely agree with you. Can you imagine if they weren't?" I asked.

There was a long pause as Nash and I both stared at the women who'd stolen our hearts. I had a feeling he was thinking exactly the same thing that was running through my mind. He confirmed that was the case when, with his voice a bit husky, he said, "I don't want to think about my life without her."

"You've had more time with Parker than I've had with Kaia, but I can't say I don't understand that. I know it might seem quick, but I swear it was like I instantly knew how much Kaia was going to change my life the moment I first laid eyes on her," I shared.

"It was the same for me with Parker," he offered. "We had our own set of issues to work through, but we're here now. And I think the only thing that's stopped her from feeling nothing but happiness has been her worry that Kaia might not find the same."

I turned my head in Nash's direction. When he looked

at me, he said, "Judging by what I've seen, I think Kaia has a real shot at getting that now."

"Thanks, man. I appreciate that."

And I did. I knew who I was, and I knew what I felt for Kaia. But hearing Nash, who had what I thought was a neutral perspective, say that he thought I could give to Kaia what he'd given to Parker was nice to hear.

What was funny about it all was that I was convinced that even though we both had so much we wanted to give to those sisters, it was really them who'd given us far more. And it seemed they did it without even trying.

Kaia

"It looks intense."

"I'm sure it's fine."

"What if it's not?"

"They'll still both be okay."

I nervously bit my lip and looked away from where Remi and Nash stood to the two women in front of me. Monroe and Parker.

Remi and Nash were far enough away that it was apparent they didn't want to be heard, and that worried me. Because if they were simply having a friendly getting-to-know-you conversation, why did they have to move so far away?

"Kaia, babe, calm down," Monroe urged. "It's really okay. My brother is more than capable of handling himself."

"Yeah, and Nash isn't a fighter," Parker reminded me.

"But they're both still protective," I reasoned. "If Nash has any doubt about Remi, he might be threatening him."

"He's not threatening him," Parker insisted through a chuckle. "He actually really likes him."

I knew that. I'd seen it. Nash had been welcoming of Remi right from the start. Sure, he asked pertinent questions, but he reserved judgment until he had all the facts. And from that point forward, he'd treated Remi like he'd known him for years.

In fact, if anyone had been hard on him, it was Parker. And even she had come around much faster than I expected.

"I know. I'm just… I've been feeling so nervous ever since we got out here," I confessed.

"What's making you feel anxious?" my sister asked.

I shrugged. "Initially, I thought it was because I knew what I had to share with you and that I was going to be meeting Monroe and her family for the first time," I offered. "But all of that is out of the way, and I'm still worried."

"Is it about Nolan?" Parker pressed.

I shook my head. "I don't think so," I answered. "I feel like it has to do with Remi. Like I'm terrified something is going to take him away from me."

"That's not going to happen," Monroe insisted. "I've seen the way Remi looks at you. Trust me when I tell you that he's not going anywhere."

I loved that she felt that way. Ever since I first met Monroe, it became clear to me just how close she was with her brother. I figured if there was anyone here right now who could read him, it was her.

"I think I'm in love with him," I blurted quietly.

"Of course, you are," Monroe said. "I could see that the first day you walked into my house with him."

I blinked in surprise.

Monroe continued, "And let me just tell you how happy that makes me. For years, I've been waiting for my brothers to settle down. Now that Remi's heading in that direction, I'm hoping Vaughn and Deacon aren't far behind."

"It's early," I remarked. "Anything could happen."

"Do you remember what happened between Nash and me?" Parker chimed in.

"Yeah."

"Okay, so you know that things can happen. That doesn't mean it'll be the end of the two of you," she assured me.

Yep, Parker had finally come around.

Shifting my gaze to hers, I asked, "How did you go from being so skeptical of him and our relationship to confident that we're going to be fine?"

With a sleeping Wren in her arms, she replied, "I can admit I had my doubts in the beginning. I think they were justified. But the truth is that he didn't back down when I expressed my concerns. And the more that I've seen him with you over the past couple of days, the more evident it's becoming just how much he cares about you, Kaia. I just wish I would have noticed sooner."

I let out a laugh. "We've only been here a couple days, Parker. How much sooner could you have noticed anything?"

Shaking her head, she declared, "No, that's not what I'm talking about. I'm referring to Nolan. I wish I would have been able to see him the way Nash did. If nothing else,

I wish my husband would have told me about the bad vibe he had. Maybe I would have noticed something and been able to talk to you about it before he had the chance to hurt you."

"Oh, don't do that to yourself, Parker," Monroe warned. "One of my best friends was being abused for years. When I finally found out the truth years after she left him, I beat myself up about it. You'll drive yourself crazy being upset about something that you can't change. Let it go, be grateful your sister got out right away, and trust that Remi will keep her safe moving forward."

Relief swept through me. I knew how guilty Parker had been feeling, and I wasn't sure how to get her to see that none of this was her fault. Hell, it wasn't even my fault. I understood the responsibility she felt because she spent her whole life looking out for me, but I didn't need her carrying this around.

Thankfully, at Monroe's suggestion, Parker seemed more willing to let it go.

I sat back, enjoying the sounds of Monroe's three oldest children and her husband playing in the pool together. I wanted to feel that. I wanted that carefree feeling of knowing life was good, and I could just sit back and enjoy it.

For the most part, I loved my life. I had my sister, Remi, my job, and my friends. It was just this one little thing nagging me that I couldn't seem to shake.

But maybe I needed to take Monroe's advice and just relax. Whatever would happen was going to happen. Sitting there worrying about a what-if or a maybe wasn't going to help.

I glanced over at Remi and Nash again and saw they

were both laughing about something. "Well, that looks much better," I muttered.

"What does?" Parker asked. She must have seen where I was looking because a moment later, she said, "Oh. Yes, that's much better."

"And see? Everyone is wonderful," Monroe added. "You were worried for no reason."

"Okay, so maybe I was overreacting about Remi and Nash," I declared.

At that moment, Remi's nephew ran up to him and asked him something. Remi nodded, set down his beer, and followed Archer to the edge of the pool. The next thing I knew, Archer was flying through the air toward his dad. Archer plunged into the pool just inches away from Stone, and when he came up for air, he squealed, "That was so much fun!"

My eyes landed on Remi again. I groaned.

"What's wrong?" Parker asked.

"Is it normal to be turned on by just the sight of your man doing nothing in particular, or is that just me?" I asked.

"Completely normal," Parker assured me.

When Monroe didn't answer, I looked over at her. Her eyes were focused on the pool, but she must have felt my stare because she looked my way.

"Oh, are you looking for an answer from me, too?" she asked. "I thought my four kids gave it away."

I giggled.

"I mean, Remi is my brother, so I'm not interested in thinking about all that, but when it comes to my man, I totally get what you're saying," she assured me.

"Good to know."

And it was. I had a feeling that Parker and Monroe were thinking about Nash and Stone in the physical sense, and I completely understood why that would be the case. It was not hard to look at either one of those men and appreciate all they had going for themselves. And they had eyes, too. They knew Remi was handsome. I was sure that's where they believed my mind was at when I asked my question.

Despite how good-looking Remi was, it had little to do with how I was feeling at the moment. I was entirely consumed by everything else that made Remi the man he was. And for that reason, I decided I needed him to know the truth. He deserved to hear what I had to say, and I found that I didn't want to keep it from him any longer.

CHAPTER 19

Kaia

TINGLES RUSHED THROUGH MY BODY WHEN STRONG, masculine hands firmly gripped the flesh on my shoulders at either side of my neck and squeezed. With his body heat close to my back, Remi's thumbs stroked down over the muscles.

"You seem like you've got something on your mind," he said softly as he continued to massage.

It was Tuesday night, and we'd gotten back to our hotel after spending our day with our sisters and their families.

As always, Remi never failed to notice when I was distracted or lost in thought.

"How do you do that?" I asked.

"Do what?" he wondered.

I felt my shoulders relax as I closed my eyes, my muscles loosening under the pressure of his hands. After letting out a soft moan of satisfaction, I answered, "You always manage to know what's happening inside my head before I can even think about opening my mouth to share anything."

Remi chuckled. "Perks of the job," he shared. "And even though I might notice that something is working inside your mind, I don't always know what it is. So, there is still some element of surprise."

I didn't respond. I continued to allow Remi to massage my shoulders. As he began to move his hands farther down my back, he asked, "Do you want to talk about it?"

"Yes," I replied. "But first, you should know that it's not anything bad that's stressing me out. That said, the massage feels really nice, so feel free to press on with that."

Remi's lips touched the skin at the side of my neck. It was so tender and sweet and sent chills down my spine.

When he pulled back a touch, he whispered, "I'll continue to massage while you share whatever you've got to share."

That right there was just another one of the things I loved about him. At the same time he used the strength in his hands to apply pressure to my back, he could also kiss me gently and speak softly.

He knew how to give me the best of everything that was him.

And it was time he knew just how much I loved and appreciated that.

"You made it easy," I finally shared.

"What?"

"Wait, no, I should first say thank you," I started. "I'm so grateful to you for coming out to Rising Sun with me so I could share the news about what's going on in my life with my sister. I know your sister and her family are here, and that gave you another reason to come on this trip. But I honestly believe you would have been here for me even if that wasn't the case."

I paused a moment as Remi's hands began working lower

and lower. Before I continued, he lifted my shirt up over my head and urged, "Lay on your belly, baby."

I got to my belly on the bed, and Remi straddled my thighs. His hands went to my ass and began kneading into the flesh.

"You're not wrong," he shared suddenly. "I would have come here whether Monroe was here or not."

"I know," I assured him. "You seem to do it so effortlessly. I know I could have come out here on my own and delivered the news to Parker, but I really appreciate knowing you have my back and support me. It means a lot, Remi."

"You're welcome, Kaia."

"So, you made it easy," I repeated.

"Parker loves you," he said. "She never would have made it difficult for you."

"That's not what I'm talking about," I declared.

His hands stopped moving, though they continued to rest on my ass. "I don't understand."

For a moment, my mind wandered into a million different places, trying to figure out the best way to share what I needed to share. When I realized I was taking too long and that it didn't matter how I said it—only that I did—I finally just came out with it.

"Falling in love."

Remi's fingers pressed into me.

I continued, "You made that easy for me, Remi. It probably wouldn't have been a surprise for me to have been completely turned off to the idea of another relationship. And though I was determined not to allow what happened to harden my heart completely, I never imagined I'd get this lucky."

"Sweetheart…" Remi trailed off, the rasp in his voice plain as day.

"I've always tried to be positive," I began again. "But I'd be lying if I said that I wasn't beginning to feel a bit hopeless when I moved out to Poppy Valley. I did my best to remain strong, but it wasn't hard to feel the doubt creeping in. Then I witnessed what happened to my sister, the profound change that happened when she met Nash, and I started to believe again. I wanted that for myself. The way she talked about Nash, I should have known that I didn't have that with Nolan. But with you, I know I do."

Remi's massaging turned to the gentle tracing of his fingertips over the bare skin on my back. A moment later, I felt his naked chest pressed against my back as his lips touched my shoulder.

"You're so sweet to me," I told him. "You make me feel special and cared for. I've never, not once in my whole life, ever had a man treat me the way that you do. You're protective and gentle. You're strong and compassionate. And more than anything else, you make me feel like you think I deserve the whole world."

Remi shifted his body off mine. He landed mostly on his belly beside me, his hand cupping the side of my face and his leg thrown over my back. His eyes boring into mine as his thumb stroked over my cheek.

"You do deserve the whole world, Kaia," he said. "And I want to give it all to you."

At that declaration, I wasn't going to hold myself back any longer.

"I love you, Remi," I rasped.

He closed his eyes and let out a deep sigh. In any other

situation, I might have thought that witnessing that was a bad thing, but seconds later, Remi shifted his body in a way that allowed him to lift mine onto his. He framed my face in his hands and crushed his mouth to mine.

His tongue swept into my mouth, tasting me, as a groan tore up his throat.

When his lips withdrew from mine, he pleaded, "Say it again."

I offered a lazy smile and whispered, "I love you."

"I love you, too, Kaia," he shared. "I've wanted to tell you that for a while now. It feels so good to finally say it."

He loved me too.

I knew it.

No man would do what Remi had done for me if he didn't truly love me.

I felt like the luckiest woman in the world.

And though there had been part of me that thought for some time that I was feeling too much too soon, deep down, I knew that wasn't the case. I'd seen enough. I'd experienced enough. Remi made me feel cherished. As I'd told him, no other man had made me feel that way.

"Hearing it is even better," I said, my mouth descending on his again.

One of Remi's hands drove into my hair as the other trailed down my back and settled on my ass. He squeezed me there and held me tight to him as he pressed his erection into me. I was wearing only a pair of panties, and Remi was wearing a pair of boxer briefs.

I loved his body.

Loved it.

I shifted myself enough so I'd be able to use my hands

and explore every inch of it. At the same time, Remi was no slouch. The feeling of his fingers running over my skin, touching me and caressing me, was everything.

He knew it, too.

Then again, there was little that Remi didn't know. It wasn't exactly like I could conceal it from him, given his impressive ability to read just about any situation. Of course, the fact that I had a hard time hiding precisely what he did to me was probably a big part of the reason he didn't have to work too hard to figure it out.

Mere moments after we started kissing, I was already worked up and feeling desperate for more of him. My mouth pulled back from his, and just inches away from his lips, I whispered, "Remi."

Like a flash, Remi flipped me to my back. His body came over mine as he began kissing down the front of my throat. One of his hands was gripping my hair at the back of my head while the other was kneading the flesh on one of my breasts.

I planted my feet into the bed, bucked my hips, and dug my nails into his shoulders.

"Remi," I repeated, my voice a deep rasp this time.

"Kaia," he returned, his voice sounding just as ragged.

"Please," I pleaded. "Fuck me, baby."

Remi's mouth had made it to my chest, but at my request, I felt his lips form a smile against my skin.

That was it.

Right there.

That was the reason Remi knew how much I loved what he was doing.

Because I would resort to begging.

Luckily, Remi being the man he was, one who seemed

incapable of denying me, lifted his body from mine, yanked my panties down my legs, and lost his boxer briefs. Seconds later, after he'd rolled a condom on, he drove inside.

Yes.

Yes!

This was it. When he gave it to me like this, all masculine, powerful, and feral, there wasn't anyone on the planet who could blame me for begging for it.

"Don't stop," I begged. "Please don't stop."

"Fuck, baby, when have I ever?" he growled as he held my hips in his hands and thrust forward with wild abandon.

He hadn't.

He never did.

Remi gave, and he gave it good. I felt like the luckiest woman alive. Coming from someone who spent the better part of her life feeling less than fortunate, that was saying something.

After driving his hips in deep for a bit while he cradled my hips in his hands, Remi pulled out, flipped me over, and lifted my ass so I was on my knees and elbows. I barely had a moment to get my bearings in the new position when Remi surged forward.

All I could do was moan.

Damn, the man was incredible.

I loved him. I loved him so much I wanted to give him back just a little bit of what he was giving me.

My fingers curled into the blanket beneath me, and I positioned my legs in a way that would give me the most leverage. Then I took over.

Remi didn't seem to mind.

In fact, once he realized that I had resolved to give some of

212

what I had to him, he took advantage and watched. Glancing back over my shoulder briefly, I saw the heated, intense look on his face as he observed our connection. Seeing it, I felt a renewed sense of determination. I looked away, smiled to myself, and continued to push back onto him.

With each movement, I felt his cock filling me from behind and his hands alternating between squeezing my ass and my hips. It was a massive turn-on, and that feeling only grew when I heard the guttural moans coming from him. He was definitely enjoying himself.

Remi was content to let me have my fun for a while, but eventually, particularly as I drew closer and closer to finding my own orgasm, he took over. Once he did, I stood no chance.

I reached out for the pillow, pulled it close, and gripped it tight.

"You going to scream for me, Kaia?"

"Remi, please," I moaned.

Remi drove in harder. Faster. Deeper.

The next thing I knew, I was screaming into the pillow as my orgasm tore through my body. My fingernails dug into the sides of the pillow. My eyes squeezed shut. And my thighs trembled on the outside of Remi's legs. Through it all, Remi delivered one deliciously punishing stroke after another until it left me, and he found his own release.

For several moments, he stayed planted to the root of his length as he bent his torso forward over mine. He peppered gentle kisses along my shoulder and upper back.

That right there did it for me. Remi went from overwhelming strength and power to the tender touch of his lips on my skin. There was nothing better.

Nothing.

"I love you, Kaia," he whispered softly.

I smiled, my eyes still closed, and returned, "I love you, too."

With that, he gave my hip a gentle squeeze as he pressed another kiss to my shoulder. Then he pulled out and moved to the bathroom to dispose of the condom. I fell to my side and couldn't wipe the sated smile from my face as I watched him walk away.

What could I say?

The view was glorious.

Remi

I closed my eyes and inhaled the scent of Kaia.

Nothing made me feel as good as being close to her like this did. Her warm, soft body was tucked tight to mine, and there was no tension running through her body. She was relaxed, sated, and sleeping soundly.

And after what we just had, it was safe to say I was feeling well beyond excellent.

Finally hearing Kaia tell me she loved me sent a whole slew of emotions that I hadn't anticipated running through me. Everything about it was better than I could have imagined.

This trip had been precisely what we both needed. Or, I assumed it was for Kaia. I knew it was for me. I think that being away from Poppy Valley for these few days gave us both an opportunity to let go of any anxiety we felt about the situation with her ex-boyfriend, especially after Kaia shared it all with her sister a few days ago. Coming to Rising Sun gave us the chance to connect with one another like we hadn't been able to when we were home with that situation swirling above us.

You made it easy.

Her words sounded in my head again. I didn't know what I did to deserve it, but I was beyond grateful that Kaia found a way to give me her heart. She had tried to give me credit for it. I understood why she might feel that way, but I honestly couldn't take the credit.

This was all Kaia.

She was such a strong, resilient woman filled with confidence like I'd never seen from a woman who had gone through even a fraction of what she'd been through.

Now she was mine in a way that meant something even more than the first time we'd slept together. Because I had her heart in my hands.

I knew it.

I knew it all along.

From the moment Kaia first walked through the doors at Archer Tactical, I knew she was someone special. With each day that passed, that feeling only got stronger. Of course, as much as I might have wanted things to end up right where they were now, I never could have imagined that she would have ended up being everything that she was to me.

There was no denying how lucky I was to have her.

And now that I was here, not long after we'd declared our love for one another, feeling the rise and fall of her chest as I cupped her breast in my hand while she slept, I felt like I was on top of the world.

I did what I could to soak up the good vibe because I had to wonder if when we finally returned to Poppy Valley if everything was going to stay this good.

CHAPTER 20

Remi

A GRUNT OF FRUSTRATION FILLED THE ROOM.

Part of me wanted to laugh because I thought it was adorable and knew she wasn't in any real danger, but I held myself back. The last thing I needed to do was frustrate her even more.

"That's not going to help you, Kaia," I pointed out. "How are you going to get out?"

She struggled a bit more, but she didn't offer any real fight or challenge to me.

It was Thursday morning, and Kaia and I were getting back into our regular routine. We made it back to Poppy Valley last night and both stayed at my place. When we got up this morning, we got ready together but drove to Archer Tactical separately.

I decided to start giving Kaia some new challenges with her training. We'd done a lot over the last several weeks, and I continued to repeat many of the same moves because I wanted to be sure she was confident in her skills.

Today, we were switching it up. And now she was on her back, pinned to the floor, with my body over hers. To say she was frustrated was an understatement.

The thing was, when Kaia first started training with me, I showed her what she needed to do before I expected her to do it. Now, I wanted to see how she'd do when confronted with a new attack. My goal was to see that she understood that physical size and strength weren't necessarily what mattered in a situation like this. It was her mindset that had everything to do with keeping herself safe.

Right now, it safe to assume her mindset was not what it needed to be. She proved that when the fight left her body, and she huffed, "It's impossible."

"It's not."

"You're heavier and stronger," she noted. "I'm not sure how I'm supposed to free myself from this position."

I brought one hand to the side of her head and tapped my finger on her temple. "You need to change your mindset," I told her. "I've told you this from the beginning. As a woman, you will almost always face an attacker who is bigger than you. You won't stand up to them if you're relying on brute strength. You need to remain focused on what you've learned."

Kaia stayed there for a moment in silence, and I could see from the look in her narrowed eyes that she was genuinely trying to assess the situation.

Suddenly, a look of understanding washed over her.

"What's happening inside that beautiful mind?" I asked.

"Well, the natural instinct I feel in this position is to push you away, but now I'm thinking that maybe that's not what I should be doing," she shared. "Maybe I need to pull you toward me so I can get you off balance and lighten the load on my hips."

A slow grin spread across my face. "Now she's thinking," I praised her. "Are you ready to try again?"

Kaia nodded.

I got myself set up in attacker mode, and almost instantly, Kaia took charge. Her hand placements weren't exactly right, but the main thing was that she'd figured out what to do and managed to get me off of her. Just as she pushed me to the side, though, I reached out and gently grabbed her hair.

"Hey!" she cried.

"You did really good, Kaia. But you want to make sure you don't keep your head this close to your attacker," I explained. "Your hair is going to be the easiest thing for him to grab when you knock him off to the side."

"That makes sense. What should I do instead?"

I fell to my back and instructed, "Climb on top of me."

Kaia cocked an eyebrow and gave me a devious look. Then she crawled on top of me like the sex kitten she was, not some scary attacker.

"Baby, I'm trying to teach you here," I reminded her. "You've got to take it easy on the seduction."

"Is that all it takes, Remi? Just a naughty look, and you're down for the count?"

I shook my head. "Nope. It's only that way with you."

Kaia smiled and lowered her mouth to mine. She offered a sweet kiss before pulling back a touch and urging, "Teach me what I've got to do."

So, I did.

And for the remainder of our time, we succeeded in staying focused on Kaia's training. I'd have been lying if I said it was easy to always keep myself absorbed in what we were doing. She was irresistible, so it took a bit more effort to get the job done. In the end, though, I was happy with how well she'd done today.

Before I knew it, our time was up, and I was walking her out to her car.

After we kissed each other goodbye and she folded into her seat, I said, "I'll see you when you get home from work tonight."

"Okay," she replied. "Thanks for waiting up for me."

"Always," I promised.

Kaia smiled and said, "I love you, Remi."

"I love you, too."

With that, I closed her door and watched her drive away. Just as her car turned out of the lot and I put my hand on the door to go back inside, I saw a familiar vehicle pull into the lot.

I held up a hand and waved as my dad pulled into a spot and parked. He made his way toward me while I waited outside for him. Once he made it over, I greeted him.

"Hey, Dad."

"Don't tell me that was her leaving as I pulled in?" he pleaded.

"What?" I returned, opening the door for us to go inside.

"Your new girlfriend," he clarified. "I thought I might catch her before she took off."

I had no idea how my dad even knew that Kaia was coming here in the mornings. It wasn't like I'd shared the information with him. Of course, I had told him that I was heading to Rising Sun for a few days with my girlfriend to visit her sister and Monroe. I wanted to make sure he could drop by Archer Tactical and lend an extra hand if the guys needed it.

"Sorry," I lamented. "If I had known you were coming, I would have asked her to stick around. Do you want me to call her and have her come back?"

He shook his head. "No, that's okay," he assured me. "Deacon and Vaughn told me about her coming here to get self-defense lessons in the mornings with you a couple times a week. I just thought I'd drop in this morning to see how your trip was and to make sure everything else was good here."

"The trip was great," I answered. "The kids have been growing like weeds."

Nodding his understanding, he replied, "Yeah, I'm going to have to plan another trip out to see them again soon. But before that happens, I'm going to warn you."

My brows pulled together. "Warn me about what?" I asked.

"Your mother," he deadpanned.

"Mom? What's going on?" I questioned him.

My dad stopped in front of me and cocked an eyebrow. "She's pissed."

My brows shot up. "Pissed?" I repeated.

"Pissed," he confirmed. "You're her firstborn, and you're finally dating. You haven't brought your girlfriend around even once to introduce us to her. And now, your mother has been on my case about it since she found out right before your trip. I thought that was bad enough. Then she talked to Monroe."

Oh no.

From what I could tell, Monroe liked Kaia. They got along great, had pleasant conversations, and even laughed a lot. Plus, they had the whole music thing in common.

"What did Monroe say?" I asked.

"Your mom called your sister earlier in the week, and

Monroe was gushing over your girlfriend," he shared, much to my relief. "Now your mom wants to meet her that much more. So, if I'm completely honest, I came here today not only to see how your trip went and to make sure everything was okay here, but I also needed to plead with you to take the time to come for a visit."

I started laughing. I knew he wasn't finding it funny, but I could only imagine how my mom was handling the news. There was no doubt that she was driving my dad insane about the fact that I hadn't come over for a visit.

"I'm sorry," I apologized through my laughter.

Shaking his head, he muttered, "I don't understand. Monroe moves away to find love and your mom is over the moon while we're all beside ourselves. You find a woman, and the only one going off the deep end is my wife. It's been how many years now, and I don't think I'll ever figure that woman out."

As comical as I found it, I didn't want my dad catching any more grief. So, I promised, "I'll call mom tonight and talk to her. Maybe I can bring Kaia by on Sunday if that works for her and for the two of you."

"Thank you."

I dipped my chin and changed the subject. "So, how was it to spend a couple days back here?" I asked. "Everything go okay while I was gone?"

"Yeah," he confirmed. "You know your brothers and the rest of the guys here had it covered."

I did. If there was one thing I never doubted, my family could pull through and pick up the slack whenever it was needed. When the time came, I'd be sure to do the same for them.

On that thought, I suggested, "Well, we should get back to it now."

My father stared at me a moment before he asked, "Does she make you happy?"

"The happiest I've ever been," I answered.

He smiled. "I'm happy for you. Your mother will be, too."

"Thanks, Dad. It means a lot."

With that, he put his hand on my shoulder, squeezed, and declared, "Now we can get to work."

And that was just what we did.

Kaia

"Did you tell her?"

I turned toward my right and saw Skylar had walked up behind me. I'd just arrived at work, my first day back since my trip to Rising Sun to visit my sister and meet Remi's.

And now that I was here, based on Skylar's question to Juan, there was clearly some news that I needed to hear.

"Tell me what?" I asked, looking between my two friends.

Juan shook his head and started, "I don't think—"

Skylar cut him off and said, "You won't believe what happened while you were gone."

This sounded exciting.

"What happened?" I wondered.

"Skylar," Juan warned.

The tone of his voice told me I was wrong. This wasn't going to be exciting. This was going to be bad news. I braced myself because, despite Juan's warning, I knew Skylar wasn't going to hold back.

"He came here," she declared.

"What? Who?" I asked. Then, before she could even open her mouth to answer me, I guessed, "Nolan?"

She nodded.

"What was he doing here? Why would he ever think it was a good idea to come here?" I asked, even though I knew neither one of them would be able to give me an answer to at least my second question.

"Maybe you should head up into the booth and get ready for your night tonight," Juan suggested.

I shot disbelieving eyes in his direction. "Are you serious?" I challenged him. "Juan, you can't keep this from me. What happened here?"

Juan offered me a sympathetic look, and a small part of me felt terrible for getting agitated with him. But this news had caught me completely off guard. I mean, I obviously learned over the last several weeks just how bad of a decision I'd made in choosing to date Nolan, but I never realized he was this stupid. Didn't he understand he could have been arrested?

The moment that thought filtered through my mind, my body tensed.

"Whoa, Banks, are you alright?" Juan asked.

I shook my head slowly as I sat down on one of the steps that led up to my booth and answered, "He doesn't care."

"What does that mean?"

"He doesn't care if he gets arrested," I clarified. "Coming here, regardless of his reason, was reckless. Please tell me he said what he wanted."

Skylar sat beside me and placed her hand on the middle of my back. "I was just as shocked as you are now that he would even dare to come to Club Infinity after what he did,"

223

she started. "I don't know what made him think he'd be welcome here either, but like you said, he doesn't seem to care."

I lifted my gaze to hers. "Does anybody know what he wanted?" I pressed.

"He knew you weren't going to be here working, so that's why he came," she said.

My brows pulled together in confusion. "That doesn't make any sense," I stated.

And it didn't. It wasn't like Nolan was the kind of guy who wanted to go out to a club regularly. In fact, this wasn't his scene at all. I should have known from the start that we wouldn't work out.

"He came here because he was hoping to talk to Bianca or me," she explained. "He got the both of us."

"Oh my God," I murmured. "I'm so sorry. What did he say?"

"It's not your fault," Skylar insisted. "And he was hoping he could convince us to talk to you for him."

"Talk to me about what?" I asked.

She shrugged. "I wish I knew," she answered. "It was at that point that Juan spotted him and made his way over to us at the bar. And just as I was about to ask him what he wanted from you, Bianca spoke."

Oh boy. Bianca was definitely the more outspoken one of my two friends. I could only imagine what she must have said to him.

"Do I even want to know?" I worried.

Skylar laughed. Juan answered, "Probably not."

Yep. I knew it. This was not going to be good.

Following a brief hesitation, Skylar shared, "Juan was just about to pull him away when Bianca called Nolan's name.

He turned back to look at her, and that's when she said that she'd love to try to convince you to talk to him, but the truth was that you'd probably be too busy having hot, steamy sex with your new man, and she'd never want to interrupt that."

"She did not."

"I told you that you didn't want to know," Juan pointed out.

Skylar nodded and confirmed, "She did. It was hysterical."

"How did he respond?" I asked.

"A strange look came over him, but he didn't really have a chance to respond," she answered. "Juan escorted him off the premises."

My eyes lifted to where Juan was standing, looking down at me. "Did he say anything to you?"

Juan shook his head. "No, but I told him he better not even think about stepping foot in this place again, or he'd be arrested for trespassing, and that would be the least of his worries."

I bit my lip.

None of this made any sense. I couldn't imagine what Nolan could possibly want from me. We were done. Finished. Over. How he could think that I'd ever want to speak with him again and why he'd ever want to show his face anywhere near me after what I'd done to him in the parking lot outside my apartment was beyond me. Then again, I probably should have expected something like this because nothing he had done since that night he first put his hands on me in anger made sense.

I stood quickly and declared, "I need to start getting myself ready for tonight."

"Kaia," Skylar called.

"It's cool," I promised. "I'm okay. I just need to work."

"Are you sure?" she asked.

I nodded.

My eyes shifted from hers to Juan's. I didn't like the look on his face. It said everything that I knew Remi's would say, too. This wasn't cool, and he didn't have a good feeling about it.

Well, that made two of us.

On that thought, I turned and climbed the stairs. A moment later, I was behind the closed door and wanted to cry.

I wasn't necessarily afraid of Nolan any longer. I didn't trust him and thought he was unpredictable. That's what bothered me. Well, that and the fact that I just wanted to be left alone. I wanted to be able to just do precisely what Bianca had said. I wanted to have hot, steamy sex with my new man. And I wanted to do that without having to think about what Nolan wanted from me.

Realizing there was nothing I could do about it at the moment, I got down to work. It didn't take long for me to get lost in the music and what I was doing. It was precisely what I needed after everything I'd just learned.

And by the end of the night, I had completely forgotten about all of it. It wasn't until I stepped out of the booth again and looked at Juan that it all came flooding back.

"Ready?" he asked.

"Yeah."

I descended the stairs. When I reached the bottom, I didn't stop to talk with him. I simply turned and moved toward the exit. Juan fell into step beside me.

He escorted me to my car, and when we got there, he asked, "You okay, Banks?"

I wasn't, but I motioned my head to indicate that I was.

"You sure?" he pressed.

"No. But I'm going home to Remi, so I know I will be," I promised.

Juan gave me an assessing look before he said, "If you need anything, don't hesitate to call me. Either one of you. Okay?"

Offering a reassuring smile, I replied, "Thanks, Juan."

With that, I got into my car and pulled away. Looking in my rearview mirror, I saw Juan watching me leave.

When I turned out of the lot, my eyes were back on the road. But I wished I would have kept my stare in the mirror just a little longer. Because then maybe I would have noticed I was being followed.

CHAPTER 21

Kaia

"**I** DON'T KNOW WHAT'S BETTER."

As soon as I revealed my dilemma, Remi cuddled closer and tightened his arm around my torso.

I was in his bed on my back, Remi's cheek was resting on my chest, and my fingernails were scratching his scalp.

"What are you choosing between?" he asked, the sleepiness still present in his voice.

"Friday nights and Saturday mornings," I answered. "I love Friday nights because I don't have to work, and we get to stay up a little later cuddling. I love Saturday mornings that you don't have to go to work because we get to sleep in together and cuddle. Though, now that I'm talking it out, maybe I should put Sunday mornings in the running, too."

Remi's hand on the arm draped across my body was resting at my side just a few inches beneath my armpit. When I finished rambling, his thumb began gently stroking the bare skin there.

Suffice it to say that after our cuddling last night while

we watched a movie, we made love. Other than the pair of panties I slipped on afterward, I was naked.

"It seems to me that it has less to do with the day and more to do with being able to spend time with one another," Remi stated.

"Yeah," I agreed.

"Is cuddling the only thing you want to do with the time we have together?" he asked.

"What do you mean?" I retorted, wondering if perhaps he wasn't enjoying how much of it we'd done lately.

There was a moment of hesitation before he explained, "It should come as no surprise that we've been spending a lot of our time indoors lately. Part of that is because I work later hours a couple nights a week, and you work very late hours a couple nights a week. But a bigger part of it, at least for me, is that when we aren't working or doing any self-defense training, all I want to do is have unhindered access to you without any other distractions."

I let out a sigh of relief. At least there was confirmation from him that he liked that time we spent together.

When I didn't immediately respond to him, he asked, "So, are there other things you'd like to do?"

"It doesn't sound much like you want to," I pointed out, my tone lighthearted and teasing.

"Kaia, just because I prefer to be naked with you doesn't mean I don't want to do anything else," he assured me. "In fact, I think it's important for us to find other things to do with one another that don't involve work or sex."

"I agree," I told him.

And I did. I mean, as much as I knew we both enjoyed that time with one another, I wasn't sure a relationship would stand the test of time if the only thing we ever did was have sex.

"What's it going to be?" he questioned me.

I thought for a minute about what I'd like to do. Then I asked, "Can we plan a day at the beach?"

I didn't have to see Remi's face to know a smile had formed on it. I felt the movement. And a moment later, he lifted his head and showed it to me.

"So I'll still get to see you mostly naked," he said, clearly distracted by the thought of me in a bikini.

"I can cover up, if you think that'd be better," I offered.

Remi shook his head. "Absolutely not."

My brows pulled together, which caused the happy look to vanish from his face and a confused expression to replace it.

Unsure of what was going through his mind and wanting to see the joy in his eyes again, I shared, "I'm surprised you're not one of those men who gets all possessive and wants me to cover my body."

The silence stretched between us as Remi stared at me. He looked dumbfounded.

"You're mine, Kaia," he deadpanned.

"Yeah?"

"So why would you think that I'm that kind of man?" he asked.

I shrugged. "I didn't mean anything bad by it, Remi," I insisted. "I just meant that you're a protective guy."

"Being protective isn't synonymous with being an ass," he countered. "That's not the kind of guy I am. Do I want other men looking at you like that? No, of course not. But it doesn't really matter if they do because you're coming home with me. Look, sweetheart, I understand that the man who should have been the most important one in your life didn't show you what he should have about how you deserve to be treated. Despite that, deep down, you already know what you deserve. That's why you walked away from your ex the minute he thought he could control you with his fists. And that's why you're here with me now. Because you know that I can and will treat you the way you deserve to be treated."

That right there was precisely the reason why I often wondered whether Remi was real or not. But I guess it made sense. It was just like he said. My father didn't show me the things he should have. He wasn't the one who made me believe I was worthy of respect. Somehow, Parker and I found a way on our own to demand it.

And Remi recognized that. I think he even respected me more for it.

"Thank you," I whispered.

"For what?"

"For being who you are," I answered.

I could have listed all that encompassed, but I'd have spent the rest of the morning talking about nothing but that.

He dropped his head forward and pressed a kiss to the top swell of my breast. When he returned his attention to my face again, he said, "I'm more than happy to plan a day at the beach with you, but I don't think it's going to happen this weekend."

"Do you have something else planned?" I asked.

"Not yet," he replied. "I wanted to talk to you about it first."

"About what?"

Remi took in a deep breath and blew it out before he said, "My dad came by Archer Tactical on Thursday right after you left. He let it be known that my mother is more than slightly displeased at the fact that I haven't made an effort to introduce you to them. She wants to meet you. They both do. And if I'm being honest, I'd like you to meet them. So, I was kind of planning to head over there tonight after you head into work to make sure my mom hasn't completely lost her mind. Then I was hoping to take you over there with me tomorrow."

My entire body froze.

He wanted me to meet his parents.

Remi wanted to introduce me to his parents. This was huge.

"Are you okay?" he asked when I didn't respond. "If it's too much too soon, it's okay. I can talk to them tonight and let them know you need more time. It's really—"

"I want to meet them," I blurted, cutting him off.

"You do?" he asked.

I nodded.

"Why did you seem so concerned?"

Shaking my head in disbelief, I promised, "I'm not concerned. I'm just really happy. We haven't been together that long, and you want me to meet them. I love that."

How could I not? The truth was, the more of Remi I got, the more I loved. Of course, part of me couldn't help from realizing just how foolish I was to miss the red flags with Nolan. We were together for nearly a year, and he never once mentioned introducing me to his family. I should have known what I was signing up for and gotten out a long time ago.

But I wasn't going to focus on that. He was no longer

part of my life. I was going to focus my attention and effort and love on the man in front of me.

"I love you," I added when he didn't respond.

He smiled at me and returned, "I love you, too." After giving me a sweet peck on the lips, he asked, "Are you hungry?"

"Yeah."

"I'll go make breakfast," he said.

"Do you mind if I give Parker a call?" I asked.

"Not at all."

"Okay. Oh, and by the way, I'm totally cool with meeting your parents on Sunday, but I did promise Skylar and Bianca that I'd get together with them that day. I'll text them now and see if we can do brunch so that we can visit your parents later in the day. Does that work?"

Remi lifted his body from mine, kissed me again, and answered, "Whatever works for you, sweetheart."

"You're the best."

With that, he exited the bed, threw on a pair of sweats, and walked out of the room. Once I was no longer distracted by the glorious sight of his naked body, I found my phone and sent a couple of texts to Bianca and Skylar, ensuring that they'd be okay with doing brunch tomorrow. Bianca replied almost immediately, confirming that it worked for her as long as it was good with Skylar. Instead of waiting around for Skylar's response, I decided to do as I told Remi I was going to do and called my sister.

"Good morning," she greeted me.

"How's my favorite girl?" I asked.

"I'm doing fantastic," Parker answered through a chuckle. "And Wren is doing great, too."

"That's good."

"What's going on? How are you doing?" she wondered.

I closed my eyes and inhaled deeply. After I let out my breath, I declared, "Remi is taking me to meet his parents tomorrow."

"Really? That's wonderful news, Kaia. How do you feel about it?" she asked.

"I don't know," I confessed. If I was being honest, I was a mix of emotions. "I'm mostly excited and looking forward to it."

"As you should be," she assured me. "Is there something that's not feeling good about it?"

With my back being supported by a couple of pillows and the bedsheet tucked under my arms as it covered my naked chest, I took a moment to consider my answer to that question.

"It's not that I don't feel good about Remi or even meeting his parents," I started. "It's more that I'm sitting here trying to come to terms with the fact that I settled for less than I deserved for so long."

The silence stretched between us. I was caught up in my thoughts and feelings while she digested the news.

When Parker finally spoke, I could hear how much she was struggling just by the sound of her voice. "I'm so happy for you," she rasped. "I know when you came out to visit and brought him with you that I was tough on him, but this is all I've ever wanted for you. And he's done everything to show me that he cares about making sure you know just what kind of man he is."

"Nolan never introduced me to his family," I declared.

"We should have known," Parker murmured.

Nodding my head, even though she couldn't see me, I agreed, "Yeah. But that's over now, and I'm honestly the happiest I've ever been in my life."

There was another pause before my sister croaked, "I'm glad he's giving that to you."

I was, too. Of course, being glad about it was one thing. Being terrified that something would happen to screw it all up and take it away from me was something else. The mere thought of not having him made my heart hurt.

"I want Remi to be that guy, Parker," I admitted. "What he does for me, how he makes me feel, and the way he treats me… I want that for the rest of my life."

"You'll have it," Parker insisted. "You said it yourself a long time ago when things started with Nash and me. Don't you remember, you told me you were too stubborn not to find your little slice of happiness? I think this is it for you."

I had said that. I only hoped she was right and the feelings I was experiencing were the real deal. Because there was no doubt in my mind that if something happened and things didn't work out with Remi, I was going to seriously struggle for the rest of my life. After having this, having the sweetness and tenderness from him that I never even knew I so desperately needed in my life, I would never want anything less than that.

I already had high standards coming into this with him. Remi just raised them a few more notches.

Just then, he peeked his head around the doorframe and said, "Breakfast is ready."

I nodded my acknowledgment, and he walked away.

"Hey, I have to go," I told Parker. "Remi just told me my breakfast was ready."

"He made you breakfast, too?" she asked.

I smiled into the phone. "Yeah."

"Kaia, I don't even know why you're worried about anything. He clearly loves you," she said.

It felt good to hear that. I liked knowing that my sister's entire perspective on Remi had changed. She did exactly as she told him she would and let me go so he could give me everything. And now that he was doing that, she could evidently see just how much he loved me.

"Yeah, he does," I returned.

"Go enjoy your breakfast and your morning with your man," she ordered. "Tell him we said hello."

"I will. You do the same with Nash and give Wren a cuddle and a kiss from me," I replied.

"Love you."

"You too, Parker."

With that, I disconnected the call and flipped the sheet off my body. I grabbed one of Remi's T-shirts and slipped it over my head. Then I made my way out to the kitchen to have breakfast with him. And I did it thinking that I needed to change my mindset.

Remi was mine. I was his. He met my sister and her family, and I'd already met all of his siblings. I was going to be meeting his parents tomorrow.

Things were good between us.

There was no reason for me to waste my time dwelling on what-if scenarios that would only break my heart. I was going to keep my mind focused on what was making me happy for as long as I had it.

I just wish I'd known I'd be at risk of losing it so soon.

My worst nightmare started that evening after work.

I had no idea what was about to happen.

I'd just finished up working for the night and packed up my things to head back to Remi's place. As usual, Juan was waiting for me when I walked out of the booth to escort me to my car.

On the way there, we even had a friendly chat. I was bubbling with excitement about finally meeting Remi's parents. Even though Juan was his typical serious self, I knew that he was happy for me deep down.

We made it to the front of my car when I stopped and turned back toward him.

As I pushed the button on my key fob to unlock my doors, I said, "I'll see you next week, Juan."

Juan confirmed he'd heard me and responded, "Stay safe, Banks."

I grinned at him and got in the car. After I buckled my seat belt and started the car, Juan stepped back and moved out of the way. And he watched as I pulled out of my spot and turned to leave the parking lot.

But it wasn't more than a full minute after I pulled out of the parking lot when I felt the cold barrel of a gun pressed to the side of my head.

When I looked in the rearview mirror, I saw that Nolan was the one holding it there.

CHAPTER 22

Kaia

TERRIFIED DIDN'T EVEN COME CLOSE TO DESCRIBING the way that I felt.

My fingers were gripping the steering wheel, my back was ramrod straight, and tension coursed through my entire body.

Blood rushed through my veins as my heart hammered wildly in my chest.

There was a gun being held to my head.

Why? Why didn't I listen to Remi and do some weapons training? Could anybody even properly prepare for something like this?

I didn't know.

What I was sure of was that I had been foolish enough to assume that this would never happen to me. Nolan had put his hands on me. He'd gotten physical. I never expected things would ever get to this level.

He didn't even own a gun. Or, at least, there hadn't been one that I'd known about when we were together. Even if he did own one, I was certain that he wouldn't have been allowed to keep it when the restraining order was put in place.

Keeping my entire body as still as possible, feeling the fear creep over me, I stayed put at the stop sign and whispered, "What are you doing?"

He pressed the gun firmly into my temple and answered, "You didn't want to listen to me before and keep your mouth shut, so now we do this my way."

A horn honked, and I jumped. There was a car behind us.

"Drive," Nolan ordered.

I put my foot on the gas pedal and pulled forward as he instructed, "You're going to do exactly what I say. Do you understand me?"

"Yes," I rasped, feeling petrified. I did not want to have my brains blown out.

For the next several minutes, which felt like hours, I listened while Nolan instructed me on where to drive. It wasn't obvious to me where we were heading based on his directions. We definitely weren't going to my place, and we weren't on our way to his either. That realization only heightened my fear.

When we'd ended up on a long stretch of road, Nolan started speaking again.

"Did you really think you could move on from me to another man just like that?" he seethed.

Oh, God.

He knew about Remi because Bianca shared it with him. I knew in her mind she had just been trying to make him jealous. Obviously, it worked. But if she had known he'd react like this, I knew she would have kept her mouth shut and never said a word.

"I know where he lives," Nolan said, his voice menacing and cold. "I followed you there two nights ago."

I swallowed hard and blinked back the tears as I tried to focus on the road. Given the time, there was very little traffic out.

This was making even less sense. We weren't heading to his place or to mine, and he followed me to Remi's place two nights ago, presumably when I left work. It was clear we weren't going there either.

"What do you want from me?" I asked.

"To make you suffer," he said. "You couldn't keep your mouth shut, and now I've got all kinds of legal problems. So, I'm just going to make this problem disappear."

Oh no. Oh, God.

Panic gripped me. Fear consumed me.

He was going to kill me.

My ex-boyfriend was going to kill me just when I thought I'd found the man who'd love me forever.

Remi.

My heart ached for him as tears slid down my cheeks. He was going to be devastated. The thought of him having to endure losing me was heartbreaking. That wasn't me being conceited. That was me knowing how a real man would feel if he lost the woman he loved.

Change your mindset.

The words Remi had said to me on multiple occasions during our training sessions rattled through my brain.

Change my mindset.

It seemed impossible. Nolan had a gun. That gun was pointed at the side of my head. There was little I could imagine being able to do that would allow me to succeed in this situation. I wasn't prepared to defend myself against someone with a gun. I didn't even know how.

Change your mindset.

I was hoping other words Remi said to me would pop into my mind because changing my mindset wasn't happening. All I could feel was dread.

"Turn left a mile up the road," Nolan's sinister voice ordered, pulling me from my thoughts. "We're going to go for a little ride first."

The freeway. I didn't know what his plan was, but I had a feeling Nolan wanted to get me far away from here before he carried out his mission. I would never be found, dead or alive.

No.

No way was I going to allow that to happen.

I was Kaia Banks. I had a sister who loved me, a niece who would look up to me, a brother-in-law who adored me, friends who cared about me, and a man who wanted to give the world to me.

I was not going down like this.

How are you going to get out?

Hope surged inside me. I changed my mindset. Now I needed to get out. I knew if I got on the freeway and drove farther and farther away from home, my chances of survival were going to diminish drastically.

I said a silent prayer before I made my move, hoping I wouldn't kill myself in my last-ditch effort to save myself.

Then I just did it and hoped for the best.

I pressed my foot on the gas a little harder and picked up speed. I did it gradually so I wouldn't alarm Nolan too soon. The closer we got to the turn, he realized I wasn't slowing down and demanded, "Slow down and turn."

I bit my lip nervously and picked up more speed, hoping he'd remain calm long enough for me to pull off my plan.

"Kaia!" he shouted.

I kept going. And at the last minute, I took the turn while bracing myself for impact.

As my car skidded off the road and went right toward the guard rail, Nolan pulled the trigger.

A loud crunch of metal and the crash of glass shattering rang through the air as the sound of a single gunshot filled my ears. Then, I heard nothing when the airbag deployed, and everything went black.

Remi

She was late.

I'd been trying not to overreact, but I had this gut feeling that something wasn't right.

Ten minutes.

It had been just ten minutes past the time that I expected Kaia to return. She was always punctual when coming home from work.

And now that I'd just attempted to call her and had gotten her voice mail, I no longer had any doubt about it. Something was wrong.

Not wanting to waste any time, I moved through my place, pulled on a pair of jeans, and slipped on some sneakers. As I made my way to the front door, I pulled up the club's phone number and tapped on the screen.

The phone rang several times before someone answered, "Club Infinity."

"Hi, can you tell me if Kaia Banks is still there?" I asked.

"I believe she's already left," the person replied.

Shit.

"Is Juan, the security guard, still there?" I pressed.

There was a brief pause. "He might be. Can you hang tight one second?"

"Sure."

I walked out, locked my door, and started heading toward the car.

"This is Juan," I heard a moment later.

"Juan, it's Remi," I said.

"Hey, man. Is everything alright?" he asked.

"I don't know. Kaia hasn't made it home yet. Did you walk her out to her car tonight?" I questioned him.

"Yeah, she left a while ago," he said. "I watched her pull out of the lot. I assume you already tried calling her?"

"No answer," I confirmed. "I'm heading out now to see if I can find her. I just don't have a good feeling about this."

There was a brief hesitation before Juan offered, "I'm walking out of here in two minutes. I'll reach out if I find her. Damn it, I don't like this. I have a feeling the guy didn't take me seriously."

"What guy?"

"Didn't Kaia tell you?" he asked. "When you two were out visiting her sister, her ex showed up here. He was trying to get her friends to convince her to talk to him."

"What? She never told me. What did they tell him?"

Juan hesitated before he hissed, "Fuck. Bianca is a bit more vocal, and because she was pissed at what the guy did to her friend, she threw out that Banks was probably too busy with you. Bianca's language was a bit more colorful and created a much more vivid picture. I don't know, Remi. I mean no disrespect when I say this to you, but think about it. If you were a man like her ex and someone told you she was fucking another man, how do you think you'd react?"

I didn't have to think about it. The thought of Kaia with another man made me feel queasy. If I felt that and had the temper that her ex had, there was no telling what I'd do. "Shit. I've got to go."

"Call me if you learn anything," Juan urged.

"Will do. Thanks."

I didn't wait for his reply as I disconnected, got into my vehicle, and pulled away. Then I called Vaughn.

Three rings later, he picked up.

"Remi?" he answered. It was clear from the sound of his voice that I'd woken him up.

"Vaughn, I think something bad might have happened to Kaia," I shared.

He was instantly alert. "What do you mean?" he asked.

I explained how she hadn't come back from work tonight and everything I'd just learned from Juan.

"I'll call Deacon, and we'll head out," he said.

"Thanks."

"None needed. She's family."

At that, we disconnected. And Vaughn's words flitted through my mind.

She's family.

She was. There was no question about it. Kaia was mine in a way that even my brothers knew it would never change. If something happened to her, I didn't know if I'd survive it.

Without any leads, I decided to take the route Kaia

would have taken to get back from work. I did this while attempting to call her again. As I suspected, she didn't answer.

The minutes passed by, the homes and businesses sliding past as I went along, and it felt like it was taking forever to get there. The streets were dead. It was the middle of the night; nobody was on the road.

Before I knew it, I made it to Club Infinity.

There was nothing.

No sign of her. No sign of anybody.

Where was she?

With no other ideas, I decided to drive to her apartment. I wasn't convinced I would find her there, but I was desperate to keep myself busy and focused on doing something to find her.

I wasn't more than two miles away from her place when my phone rang.

"Vaughn?" I answered.

"Deacon found her," he said.

My chest decompressed as the air rushed from my lungs. I hadn't realized I'd barely been breathing the whole time until that moment.

"Where is she?" I asked.

I was met with silence.

"Vaughn?" I called.

"We're just off the on-ramp to the freeway at Newton Road," he said.

Not wasting a second, I whipped my car around and headed in that direction. "I'm on my way," I declared. "She's okay? What happened?"

"Brace yourself, Remi," Vaughn warned.

"Why? Is she okay?" I pressed, desperation consuming me.

"Physically speaking, she's going to be okay," he said. "But mentally… Remi, you need to get here. Deacon's with her, but she's distraught. Her ex was in her car, and he had a loaded gun pointed at her head the entire time."

"Fuck… fuck!" I barked.

"Just get here."

"I'm on my way. Where is he?" I snapped.

"In the ambulance," Vaughn told me. "Police are here as well."

Why the hell was he in an ambulance? What happened? What about Kaia?

"I'll be there in a few minutes. Tell her I'm coming."

"Got it."

I disconnected and tossed my phone into the passenger seat. Then I raced to the location where Vaughn said they were.

Even though I was only minutes away, it felt like it was taking hours in a race to get to her. I didn't know what I'd find when I arrived, but I knew it would be awful. If Vaughn was warning me to brace myself before I got there, it was almost inevitable that I'd have a hard time controlling my reaction when I saw her and learned about whatever it was that she went through.

He had a loaded gun pointed at her head.

Kaia.

My sweet, strong, beautiful girl.

Finally, when I was about a quarter mile away from where Vaughn told me to meet them, I saw the lights. Police. Fire. Ambulance.

I got as close as I could since the roads were blocked off and ran the rest of the way there.

"Whoa," one of the officers said.

"My girlfriend was in the car," I shouted to the officer I'd never met before.

A moment later, a familiar face appeared and said, "He's good, Officer Garcia. Remi's the owner of Archer Tactical. He runs a lot of training for some of our guys."

Officer Garcia let me through, and that's when I saw it.

Kaia's car had plowed into the guardrail. If that wasn't enough to make me feel sick with worry, the obvious bullet hole in her window would have done the trick.

All I could think about was her.

My eyes left the vehicle, scanned the area, and found Deacon sitting in the back of an ambulance with Kaia wrapped in his arms. Standing next to them just outside the ambulance was Vaughn, who looked in my direction and locked eyes with me. I watched his mouth move. Barely a second later, Deacon's gaze shifted to mine.

Kaia didn't move.

Or, she didn't until Deacon bent his head and whispered something in her ear.

Slowly, Kaia pulled her face from his chest and looked up at him. Her eyes followed his stare until she found me. For several seconds, neither one of us moved. Then it felt like we were in a movie.

I took off running toward her as Kaia leaped out of Deacon's arms and came charging toward me. Her body collided with mine as she threw her arms around my neck and burst into tears.

"It's okay, sweetheart. I've got you now," I tried to comfort her.

She cried harder and held on tighter. "I… I… I thought I was going to die."

Fuck.

"You're here, baby. You're alive. You're okay."

"P… Please, Remi," she pleaded.

"What, Kaia? What do you need, sweetheart?" I asked her. I would have given her anything she needed right then and there. I didn't care what it was.

"Please don't ever let me go," she begged.

My arms tightened around her. "I'm never letting you go, baby," I whispered.

For the next several minutes, Kaia and I didn't say anything. I was giving her the time she needed to collect herself and pull it together. If it took her until the sun came up, so be it. I'd stand here until she indicated it was okay to loosen my hold on her.

Eventually, well before the sun came up, Kaia pulled her face from my neck and looked up at me. I searched her face, illuminated by the lights from the police cars, fire trucks, and ambulances.

Now that she'd settled down, I needed to ask her some questions.

"Were you hurt?" I asked.

She shook her head. "The force of the airbag knocked me out, but otherwise, I'm okay," she answered.

"Nothing hurts? Are you sure?"

Kaia nodded. "I just want to go home with you."

"Did you talk to the officers yet?" I asked.

"I started to, but then I lost it. Vaughn took over and told them about Nolan."

I wanted to know what happened, but I didn't want to put her through more turmoil right now. "When you're ready to talk to me about what happened, I'm ready to listen, okay?"

"Yeah," she rasped.

Just then, Deacon and Vaughn walked up.

"How did you find her?" I asked Deacon.

"Police scanner," he answered.

I lifted my chin in understanding. My eyes slid to the ambulance I was certain Kaia's ex was in. I didn't want to ask anything specific while she was in my arms, but I hoped my brothers could read the curiosity in my expression.

Thankfully, they did. Vaughn shared, "Kaia's a determined woman. She made a split-second decision to crash the car in an effort to save herself. Luckily, she was wearing her seat belt, so she was okay. Her back seat passenger was not as fortunate. He's heading to the hospital with a couple of officers in tow because once he recovers from the physical damage he experienced, he's going straight to jail."

My arms tightened around her as my gaze dropped to hers. "I'm proud of you, Kaia."

She offered a small smile before burying her face in my chest. I held her close, offering what comfort I could.

Dropping my head so my mouth was at her ear, I suggested, "Let's see what we've got to do so we can get out of here and get you home, okay?"

"Yeah," she replied.

With that, I loosened my hold on her so we could do just that.

But one thing I didn't do was leave her side.

CHAPTER 23

Kaia

BANG. BANG. BANG.

The sound of a gunshot rang in my ears.

I gasped and clutched my hand to my chest as my body flew forward and my eyes opened. I woke up completely out of breath.

Barely a moment later, a delicate touch landed on the middle of my back, causing me to tense up. No sooner did I tense up when I was able to relax because I heard his voice.

"It was just a dream. You're okay, Kaia," Remi said.

I let out a sigh of relief and leaned my torso into him.

His arms came around me as he fell to his back in his bed. Remi held on tight and whispered calming words in my ear.

It was Monday night, or perhaps early Tuesday morning, and suffice it to say I hadn't fully recovered from my whole ordeal with Nolan from a couple nights ago. During the day, I did okay. I had my moments, but for the most part, I'd been doing alright.

For the last two nights, though, sleep hadn't been easy.

On Sunday night, I tossed and turned and found it difficult to find rest even though I was utterly exhausted. And now, it seemed as though I was going to be dealing with flashbacks.

"I can't forget that sound," I finally confessed, my voice raspy from just being woken up.

"What sound, sweetheart?" Remi asked.

"The gunshot. I can hear it like it's still happening right here beside me," I told him.

His arms tightened around me. "You're safe," he reminded me. "He can't come near you again. And I'm not leaving your side. I'd never let anything happen to you."

"I know. I just can't seem to get away from that sound."

Remi kept one arm wrapped firmly around my waist while the other hand drifted slowly up my back until it was in my hair. As he ran his fingers through my strands, he reasoned, "It's only been a couple days, Kaia. I promise it'll get better. I'll do whatever I have to do to make sure of that. You don't have to be afraid."

I loved that.

Even still, I needed him to understand.

And since the extent of what I'd shared with him hadn't been more than what I'd shared with the police, which was merely an accounting of what happened that night from the time I left Club Infinity until the time they arrived on the scene, I figured there was no better time than the present.

Remi had been patient and understanding.

He didn't even go to work on Monday morning because he wanted to be there for me if I needed him. Beyond what he had gotten from me when I first saw him that night and ran into his arms, I hadn't given him any insight into how my heart and mind were handling it.

And not once since he brought me back to his place after it all went down did he pry for more information. He had given me the time to deal with it independently, but he also made it clear that he was there whenever I was ready to share.

I was ready to share now.

"It was the same both times," I murmured.

"What was the same?" he countered.

I took in a deep breath and prepared myself to share the rest. It wasn't going to be easy for me to reveal the rest, just as I believed it would be difficult for Remi to hear it. Despite that, I knew he'd want it. He'd do anything to help ease the burden I was feeling. The only thing was, I wasn't convinced there was anything he could do to make this particular thing any better for me. If nothing else, I thought it could help me if I got it off my chest, so it was worth a shot.

"Both times he tried to kill me, I wasn't thinking about myself," I started. "That first time, in my apartment with the knife at my throat, all I could think about was Parker, Wren, and Nash. I didn't want to die because I didn't want them to suffer any heartache. The same thing happened this time. Except, this time, I didn't just think about my sister and her family. They came into my thoughts, but it was you who was at the forefront of my mind."

"Sweetheart…" Remi trailed off.

"I was terrified that I was going to die, and you were going to be devastated," I went on. "My heart hurt so much thinking about you suffering through that kind of pain. I knew that if the roles were reversed and I lost you, I'd never be the same again. I didn't want you to have to go through that."

His fingers pressed in.

"Christ," he rasped.

The sound of his voice told me I'd made the right decision that night. He wouldn't have handled losing me very well at all.

"Purposely crashing that car was the only thing I could think to do to save myself in that situation," I told him. "I knew there was a chance I could have been seriously hurt or worse, but I figured that was better than the alternative, which was certainly going to be a death sentence."

I paused a moment to allow Remi to speak. It took him a moment, but with a voice that had dipped so low it was just a touch over a whisper, he eventually declared, "I'm so proud of you, Kaia. You did exactly what you should have done in that situation. You found a way to get yourself out of it. And yes, it was a risk, but it was a calculated one. When you found yourself in the line of fire, you did what you had to do to save yourself. I couldn't have asked for anything more."

"I don't ever want to live without you, Remi," I rasped as a tear leaked from my eye and fell to his bare chest.

Remi gave my hair a gentle tug before he brought both of his hands to either side of my face. Stroking his thumbs along my cheeks, wiping away my tears, he insisted, "Baby, I'm not going anywhere. And you've clearly proven you're determined to stick around."

"I was so scared," I whispered.

His hands slid back into my hair and came around my body. He hugged me tight and returned, "I know. I was, too."

I couldn't even imagine what he must have been feeling when he realized something was wrong. Remi was far too observant, so it was no surprise he acted as quickly as he did.

"Thank you for calling your brothers," I said. "I would have preferred that your face was the first familiar one I saw after all of that, but since it couldn't be you, I'm glad it was Deacon's."

"Me too."

For a long time, I stayed there like that with Remi. Neither of us said anything. We simply held on because we both understood that having each other there was all that mattered.

Following an extended pause, I shared, "I think I'd like to start weapons training."

"Kaia, I'll teach you everything you want to know, but I hope you understand he can't come after you again," Remi replied.

He couldn't come after me again. I knew that. For the first time in my life, it was proven to me that this type of thing would be taken seriously. Sure, at the time I'd experienced abuse before, my sister and I were just kids. And while I had her willing to stand up for me and protect me, she didn't have anyone. No adult stepped up to the plate and rescued the two of us collectively. Now, I finally had that, and it felt like the greatest reward.

"I know. And I'm not saying I'm looking to start carrying something around right now, but I want a better understanding of how to handle them," I explained. "I don't want to feel helpless like that again."

"You're far from helpless," Remi assured me.

I loved that he felt that way, and a big part of me knew he was right. I still didn't think it was a bad idea to have some knowledge of the weapon whose sound was capable of waking me from my sleep days after I'd heard it.

"Thank you for listening to me," I whispered, following a long stretch of silence.

"Anything you need, I'll do my best to give it to you," he remarked as he loosened his hold and started trailing his fingertips lazily up and down my spine.

"Will you be there with me when I call Parker later to tell her what happened?" I asked.

"You know I will," Remi responded, not once faltering in delivering comforting strokes of his fingers over my skin.

Within minutes, wrapped up in the warmth and security of his embrace, I fell back asleep.

Two weeks later

"I'm doing much better."

Silence came through the phone line for a long while before Parker finally replied, "I've been so worried about you."

She hadn't attempted to hide that fact. I hated that for her, but I also couldn't hide what happened to me from her.

I told Parker about what Nolan did, and suffice it to say that she nearly lost her mind. Ever since, I wasn't exactly sure who had had a more difficult time in getting past it all. The minute I called my sister and told her the whole story, she immediately declared that she was going to fly out to see me. I insisted that she not do that and assured her I was okay.

It wasn't a complete lie. I was okay, even if I had still been struggling at the time. The extent of my struggle with everything had mostly been me waking up in the middle of the night. Over the last week, that had all subsided.

Nolan was taken into custody and was mostly a distant memory for me now. In fact, if it weren't for the fact that my sister was still so concerned about me, I probably wouldn't have spent so much time thinking about the guy.

I believed that a big part of why I managed to recover so quickly was because I had Remi. He had been nothing but supportive and gentle. When I needed to talk, he lent a listening ear, and when I needed a comforting embrace, he wrapped his arms lovingly around me. And every night that I did wake up because I could still hear the gunshots, he woke with me. Sometimes I needed to talk about it, and other times I just needed to know he was there with me. No matter what, Remi stayed awake with me and didn't fall back asleep until I drifted first.

I was beyond lucky to have him.

While he was here in Poppy Valley with me and could see the improvements I'd made over the last two weeks, Parker couldn't. So, I understood why she was having such a hard time.

"I promise you don't have to be worried anymore," I assured her. "In fact, I'm getting myself back to doing normal things, even some scary things."

"Scary?" she worried.

I let out a laugh.

"Well, one of the normal things I did was get together with Bianca and Skylar about a week ago," I started. "It was nice to do that and finally have the chance to sit down and tell them the whole story. The scary thing I did was finally meeting Remi's parents."

"Oh, what a relief," Parker declared. "I thought you were referring to something serious. How did meeting the parents go?"

"Really, really great," I answered. "They were so kind and

welcoming. Almost immediately, it became clear why Remi is the guy that he is."

"What do you mean?" she asked.

I smiled just thinking about it. I wasn't sure Remi could have asked for better parents than the ones he got.

"He gets his protective nature from his dad," I explained. "Watching Remi's father with Remi's mom was so heartwarming. That man would move mountains for his wife. And Remi gets his kindness and compassion from her. She was such a wonderful woman."

I paused briefly as the thought I'd had the same night I met Remi's parents filtered back into my mind.

"I wonder what she would have been like?" I murmured.

"What? Who?" Parker questioned me.

"Mom," I clarified. "If she hadn't passed away, would our mother have been like Remi's? Would our father have turned into the monster that he did?"

Parker audibly sighed. "We're never going to know that, Kaia," she rasped. "Regardless, I think we did okay for ourselves in the end."

"Yeah," I agreed. "It was all thanks to you, you know? I never would have survived him all those years ago if it hadn't been for you sacrificing the way you did. I'll never be able to thank you enough for everything you did to protect me."

The silence stretched between us briefly before Parker insisted gently, "I'd do it all over again in a heartbeat for you. And just so you know, you've already thanked me."

"How?"

I could hear the pride in her voice as she answered, "When you stood up for yourself and got out of that relationship. When you demanded better for yourself. When you didn't lock your heart down from the possibility of finding love. And when you found a good man and let him give you everything you deserve."

"Parker..." I trailed off.

"It's the truth, Kaia. That's all I've ever wanted for you."

Once again, I was reminded of just how lucky I was. Not only did I have Remi, but I also had Parker. They were all that I needed. Fortunately for me, I got more. I got Nash, Wren, Deacon, Vaughn, Monroe, her family, and Remi's parents. Plus, I had Juan, Skylar, and Bianca.

Maybe I didn't have my parents. Perhaps I would find myself wondering from time to time what life might have been like if my mother never died, but I still managed to find a family that was all my own.

If things had been different, I might not have ended up in California. And it was very likely I never would have met Remi. My life was what it was. I'd gotten through a lot, and I was happy. There was nothing left for me to complain about.

On that thought, I was about to change the subject, but my sister beat me to it.

"There are only one or two more things that could make me even happier," she announced.

I'd do anything to try and make Parker happy, so I replied, "Anything at all. What is it? Do you need me to come out for another visit?"

Parker let out a laugh and said, "You know I'd never discourage you from doing that, but I was thinking of something else."

"What is it?" I wondered.

"I'd love to see you married with some kids," she shared. "I want my own niece or nephew to spoil."

Married with kids. The thought speared through me, and hope filled my heart.

Could I be married with kids? More importantly, would that happen with Remi? As soon as she said it, it became a real possibility in my mind. And now I realized how much I wanted it. I'd always been the one, out of the two of us, who was more determined to find that level of happiness, so it seemed only natural that I would have thought about it with Remi. But with everything I'd been dealing with regarding Nolan, I had to face the fact that a small part of me might have started giving up hope.

Married with kids.

"It's a little early," I started. "I'm not sure I'm ready for children just yet, but Remi is a man I could definitely see myself with for the long haul. For now, I'm happy to just be the two of us while we take the time to get to know one another a little better without protective orders and a crazy, abusive ex-boyfriend hanging over our heads."

"I hope Remi's the one for you, Kaia," Parker said. "I want you to always be as happy as you were when you came here with him."

"I want that, too."

The silence began to settle between us for a moment, and I had a feeling we were both letting the reality of our lives sink in. We'd come so far from the two girls we used to be. It meant something that we managed to get to the place we were now, and moving forward in both love and parenthood, I knew we'd both continue to strive to give ourselves the very best.

Fortunately for us, we wouldn't need to do it alone. Because Parker had Nash, and I had Remi.

Yep.

There was no doubt about it. We were strong women who had found a way to give ourselves the life we deserved.

On that thought, I couldn't help but think about our ability to raise daughters who could do the same. I'd have it one day, and in the meantime, I'd watch as my sister gave it to Wren.

Visions of my niece popped into my head, and I asked, "How's my favorite little girl doing?"

"She's happy as can be," Parker started.

Then she went on to tell me about all things Wren.

And when I finished the call with my sister, I couldn't stop myself from thinking about my future. When I did, all I could see was Remi, which put a smile on my face.

EPILOGUE

Remi

I WAS A FEW MINUTES AWAY FROM COMPLETELY LOSING my cool.

Part of me wanted to laugh at myself. I mean, before Kaia came into my life, there hadn't ever been a situation I was in that made me feel like this. I had always been calm, rational, and ready for anything.

Now, I was anything but.

Now, I was filled with nerves, feeling a little crazy and a lot unprepared.

I shouldn't have been surprised by any of this, considering nothing about my life had been typical since she came into it. In any other case, any different scenario, feeling like this would cause a lot of stress, it didn't when it came to Kaia.

I liked it.

I liked knowing this woman kept me guessing. In some strange way, I looked forward to not knowing whatever might come next with her.

Only, at this moment, the unknown left me feeling slightly intimidated.

This was quick, much faster than I would have ever anticipated. And yet, at the same time, it didn't feel like it was happening soon enough.

It was a Friday, New Year's Eve, and I'd decided to finally pop the question. I wanted to head into the new year with Kaia as my fiancée. I wanted her to know how much she meant to me and that I was never going to let her go.

For the better part of the last week, we'd debated about how to spend the night. Or, Kaia did.

Anyone looking for a night out would not have been disappointed if they chose to go to Club Infinity. It was sure to be a great time there.

But since that was where Kaia worked, and I knew what I had wanted to do tonight, I eventually told her I was okay with simply having a quiet night in. Surprisingly, she didn't have any issue with it.

Then again, we'd had some pretty busy weeks over the last couple of weeks. Between the holidays with my family, visiting her sister and her family, as well as Monroe and her family in Rising Sun, Kaia and I hadn't had a whole lot of uninterrupted time alone with one another.

We didn't mind the time with our families, obviously. But it was safe to say that we were both looking forward to some time alone with one another.

It being the holiday worked in my favor. Since we were staying in, I wanted to make sure that everything was perfect for Kaia. So, she didn't bat an eyelash when I told her that since it was our first New Year's Eve together that I still wanted it to be special.

She was beyond excited about it and told me she'd go back to her apartment, get herself all dolled up, and I could pick her up. That was the only good thing about the fact that Kaia still hadn't given up her apartment. After this, though, we were going to have to work on that.

I'd spent most of the afternoon getting everything prepared, and now I was on my way to pick her up.

The closer I got to her place, something inside me changed. The strange thing about it was that I suddenly realized that I wasn't feeling nervous. That's when it hit me that it wasn't necessarily fear about how tonight would go. This was all about feeling excitement and anticipation.

Kaia was going to officially be mine.

I knew it.

Feeling worried about how she'd react was foolish. Kaia and I loved each other, she'd been through hell, and we managed to come out the other side even stronger together. We were meant for one another.

I finally arrived at Kaia's place and knocked on her door. Seconds later, she was standing in front of me in a slinky silver dress that showed a lot of skin. Her feet were in a pair of heels that made her already long legs look even longer.

"Sweetheart, you look amazing," I immediately declared.

Kaia beamed at me. "Thank you. I thought you might like this dress."

"I love it almost as much as I love you," I told her.

And it was the truth. That dress was made for Kaia's body. With the amount of skin she was showing, I was glad we weren't going to be going out anywhere. That had nothing to do with being insecure about other men seeing her like this. She was with me, so that didn't bother me. What made me happy about not going out was not having to worry about how long I'd have to wait for us to leave so I could get her home and out of that dress.

"You look handsome," Kaia announced.

I returned the smile and asked, "Are you ready to go?"

"Yeah."

A few minutes later, we were in my car on the way back to my place. I was doing my best to remain unaffected by what was ahead, but it wasn't easy.

Luckily, Kaia helped by filling the ride with conversation.

"You know, I really would not have minded making us dinner tonight," Kaia shared.

"I know, baby, but I wanted to do something special for you," I told her.

"When am I going to be able to do something special for you?" she asked.

In just a little bit, I thought.

"I'm sure you'll have your chance," I answered.

Kaia grunted in a way that told me she didn't exactly believe what I was telling her. All I could do was laugh.

Before I knew it, we had made it back to my place. As I got out of the car and rounded it to meet Kaia on her side, I felt like my heart was going to beat right out of my chest.

Kaia placed her hand in mine and stood up when I opened her door. I led her to the house and opened the door. Ushering her inside ahead of me, I braced myself for a reaction.

"Remi…" Kaia trailed off, her voice just a touch over a whisper.

It had worked. I'd pulled it off. Or, at least, I'd pulled off the surprise portion of it.

Kaia stepped carefully, not wanting to trample the rose petals I'd lined the floor with. I held on to her hand and kept her steady until she came to a stop in the great room. When she did, her stunned eyes came to mine.

"What is all this?" she whispered.

Taking both of her hands in mine, I searched her beautiful face and smiled. Damn, how lucky was I? She was the most beautiful woman in the world.

"Kaia, sweetheart, you've changed my life," I started. Tears instantly filled her eyes. I continued, "I know it hasn't even been six months since I've met you, but I don't care. I have no desire to wait any longer. I know you're the one for me. You've made me happier than I ever thought possible, and there isn't anything I wouldn't do to show you just how much I love you. I want to be the man in your life that you can always depend on to love, honor, respect, and protect you. With everything I have, Kaia, I'll always protect you."

I picked up the ring box I had sitting on the rose-covered coffee table, got down on one knee, and looked up at her.

"I love you with all my heart, Kaia Banks. Will you marry me?"

Kaia nodded her head several times before she rasped, "Yes, Remington Archer, I'll marry you."

With her answer, I slipped the ring on Kaia's finger before I stood up and wrapped my arms around her waist. She instantly buried her face in my neck at threw her arms over my shoulders.

"I love you so much," she cried. "You are the best thing that's ever happened to me."

"I feel the same way about you," I told her.

Kaia held on for a long time before she pulled her face

back, looked at me, and shared, "No other man has ever treated me the way that you do. And if I'm completely honest, I'd go through everything I've gone through a hundred times over if it meant that I'd get the privilege of being loved by you."

I lifted my hand to the side of her face, stroked my thumb along her jaw, and promised, "And if I had known about you all along, there isn't anywhere I wouldn't have gone to be able to save you from all of that heartache. I meant what I said, sweetheart; I'll do whatever it takes to protect you."

"I know you will."

Seconds later, she leaned forward and touched her mouth to mine. I quickly took over the kiss, and the next thing I knew, I was making love to my future wife on a bed of rose petals. It was, by far, the best way to end the year. Even better, hours after I'd fed her dinner, when the clock struck midnight, I made love to her again and thought that there was no better way to start a new year.

Kaia was going to be mine forever, and I couldn't wait to see what our future held.

ACKNOWLEDGMENTS

To my husband, Jeff—There are never enough words to tell you just how much all of your love and support mean to me. I couldn't do this without you. Thank you for always having my back. I love you.

To my boys, J&J—I don't know if you'll ever understand just how much I love you both. The two of you are my reason for everything. I love you.

To my ARC readers—THANK YOU! I know I'm shouting, but I can't help it. You all mean so much to me. Thank you for supporting me and sharing your love for my books.

To my team, Sarah, Stacey, Ellie, & Rosa—My books wouldn't be half as good as they are without all of you. Thank you for unparalleled support and dedication. I so appreciate you all.

To my loyal readers—I could cry just thinking about how happy I am to have you reading my books. There is so much love and enthusiasm for my stories and my characters, and I can't even begin to find the words to tell you what it means to me. Thank you, thank you, thank you. To each and every single one of you, from the bottom of my heart... I sending you all my love.

To the bloggers—Thank you for supporting my work. Whether this was your first, fifth, or twenty-fifth book of mine that you shared, read, or reviewed, it never ceases to amaze me how many people there are willing to help spread the word. Thank you for joining me on this journey and being part of the success of each of my books.

OTHER BOOKS BY
A.K. EVANS

The Everything Series
Everything I Need
Everything I Have
Everything I Want
Everything I Love
Everything I Give

The Cunningham Security Series
Obsessed

Overcome

Desperate

Solitude

Burned

Unworthy

Surrender

Betrayed

Revived

ABOUT
A.K. EVANS

A.K. Evans is a contemporary romance author of over twenty published novels. While she enjoys writing a good romantic suspense novel, Andrea's favorite books to write have been her extreme sports romances. That might have something to do with the fact that she, along with her husband and two sons, can't get enough of extreme sports.

Before becoming a writer, Andrea did a brief stint in the insurance and financial services industry and managed her husband's performance automotive business. That love of extreme sports? She used to drive race cars!

When Andrea isn't writing, she can be found homeschooling her two sons, doing yoga, snowboarding, reading, or traveling with her family. She and her husband are currently taking road trips throughout the country to visit all 50 states with their boys.

For new release updates, sign up for the A.K. Evans
newsletter: eepurl.com/dmeo6z

Be sure to follow Andrea on all social media platforms, too.

Facebook:
www.facebook.com/authorAKEvans

Facebook Reader Group
http://bit.ly/2ys50mU

Instagram
www.instagram.com/authorakevans

Goodreads Author Page
www.goodreads.com/user/show/64525877-a-k-evans

Bookbub:
www.bookbub.com/authors/a-k-evans

Twitter:
twitter.com/AuthorAKEvans

Made in the USA
Las Vegas, NV
21 August 2021

28622772R00163